"Do you know what that ring stands for, Julianne?"

Julianne looked at the ring in question. "It means I'm your wife."

Caleb reached across the table to capture her hand. "What else does it mean to you?"

She tugged on her hand but Caleb refused to release her. "It means I am to do anything you ask me to," she whispered, and lowered her lashes.

Caleb rubbed the back of her hand with his thumb. "Julianne, we are married. You are not my slave, and I'm not your master. We are partners, and someday I hope that we will be best friends."

He watched a tear trickle down her face. "That ring means more to me than you will ever know. It means you are my wife, my friend and the woman who holds my heart."

Her head snapped up. "You don't love me."

"You're right. But I plan to."

Jean Kincaid can be found most mornings knee-deep in devotionals and day planners. She loves the early hours spent with the Lord. Jean speaks at ladies' retreats and women's events, and enjoys all things mission related. Her heart's desire is to create stories that will draw people to a saving knowledge of our Lord Jesus Christ.

Books by Jean Kincaid

Love Inspired Heartsong Presents

The Marriage Ultimatum
A Home in His Heart
Wedding at the Hacienda
The Lumberjack's Bride

JEAN KINCAID

The Lumberjack's Bride

HEARTSONG
PRESENTS

Recycling programs
for this product may
not exist in your area.

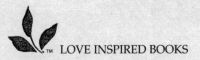 LOVE INSPIRED BOOKS

ISBN-13: 978-0-373-48776-9

The Lumberjack's Bride

www.Harlequin.com

Printed in U.S.A.

And above all things have fervent love for one another, for love will cover a multitude of sins.
—*1 Peter* 4:8

To my sisters, Sherlene Watson and Martha Taylor.
A threefold cord is not easily broken.
So thankful for you both.

Chapter 1

Logging camp outside Seattle,
Washington, 1866

"I'll give you eighty dollars for the little lady, Sloan!"

"No! I'll pay you one hundred dollars. You owe me, Sloan." Judging by the speaker's rotten teeth and tattered clothing, Julianne Maxwell figured it had to be a gambling debt Sloan owed him, for the man's appearance definitely was not that of a banker.

She grew hot with resentment and humiliation as the loggers auctioned her off like a milk cow at a Saturday farm sale. Her annoyance increased when she found her hands shaking. What had she done?

When she'd made plans to escape from New York, Seattle had seemed the perfect place to settle down. She'd arrived in Puget Sound four days ago, traveled on

Skid Road through the Duwamp town, and now here she stood, smack in the middle of a logging camp in the biggest mess of her life, bar none.

Weariness enveloped her as she tried to concentrate. It appeared her day of reckoning could be postponed no longer.

The men crowded closer, and the air thickened with tension. Never in all her born days had Julianne smelled so much sweat, dirt and foul breath all in one small space. She took a step backward only to find the men had closed in on her from behind. She searched the crowd for the only person familiar to her; a woman named Maggie who had given her a ride from town.

"What in blue blazes is going on here? Why aren't you men working?" The loud voice parted the sea of soiled bodies, and the large man attached to it made his way to her. With an ax propped on his shoulder, he looked down his eagle nose and continued to demand answers. "What's the cause of this ruckus, Sloan?"

Julianne chanced a look at the man who stood by her side. Sloan Kellywood twisted his hat in his hands and refused to answer.

"I'll tell you what's going on here." A woman's voice rose as she pushed her way through the crowd. Maggie. *Thank You, God.* "This no-good-for-nothing mule of a man ordered himself a bride, then up and married one of the Skid Road girls in town. That's what's happened. Now his mail-order bride shows up, and he doesn't want her."

Maggie stopped in front of Sloan. She pushed a bony finger into his chest. "He's selling her off like she's his personal property or something."

Conscious of intense scrutiny as every eye looked

her over from head to toe, Julianne felt sure her face had just caught fire.

The big man spoke to Sloan. "What gives you the right to sell this woman?"

"She owes me for the ship fare. And I want my money, boss. She owes me." Sloan's voice rose in anger. He stepped away from Maggie's abusing finger.

Julianne watched Sloan puff out his chest. How could she have believed his letters? This was not the man who had written to her. He just couldn't be. While his words hadn't been flowery, that man had shown kindness in his words. She fought back tears of disappointment.

"Now let me get this straight, Sloan. You sent for her; she came. Did you send a wire telling her you were already married and that she should return the money?"

"No, boss…"

The boss interrupted Sloan, his impatience with the matter evident in the expression of disbelief on his face. "Then she followed your orders. She's arrived and you don't get your money back." The tone of his voice said, *and that's final.*

"But she didn't even bring a trunk, boss. There wuz no boxes nor nuthin'. Just her satchel of clothes." The man's whining voice set Julianne's teeth on edge. A valise with a few personal possessions was all she'd had time to pack.

"What in thunder are you talking about, Sloan?" The big man dropped the ax from his shoulder to the ground and leaned on the handle, his chin jutted forward, a less than subtle threat to Sloan that he'd better clear things up in a hurry.

"I sent an extra hundred, Boss, for her truesole. Took me nigh on to a year to save that money."

"Her what?"

If her circumstances had not been so dire, Julianne would have laughed at the look on the boss's face.

"Trousseau," Maggie corrected Sloan, then she turned her gaze on Julianne as if she, too, wondered why Julianne had arrived so lacking in possessions.

"I was expecting her to bring some of them fancy linens from New York. You know, boss. Towels, sheets and curtains to outfit my new home. Maybe some good pots and pans to cook with. And she was supposed to buy several fine dresses and material to make more. I paid to have all that frippery, but she showed up empty handed, with just that old valise."

Julianne about swallowed her tongue. She'd never heard a man lie so outright before.

"What do you have to say about this?" The boss turned to her and demanded answers in the same booming voice he'd used on Sloan.

Now wasn't the time to turn into a weeping female, Julianne told herself. She pulled her shoulders back, forced herself to stand tall, and answered as honestly as she knew how. "I'm confused, sir. I don't know what he's talking about. I didn't receive any money, just a letter saying to come. So…I signed on with Asa Mercer, the man who brings out brides for men in remote areas of the west. When I explained to him that I was betrothed to a man in the area and didn't have the means to get here, Mr. Mercer agreed to let me travel with them. He paid my fare."

"You liar! I sent the money for your ticket!" Sloan swept his arm upward to strike her.

Julianne cringed and stepped back. The heat and stench of unwashed bodies at her back halted her retreat.

When no blow came, she opened her eyes and looked at Sloan under the cover of her eyelashes.

The big man held Sloan by the front of his shirt. His angry voice rumbled over them like hot lava. "No man hits a woman in my camp." He growled in Sloan's face, then shoved him away. He turned his gaze upon her, his dark brows slanted in a frown.

"Sir, I never received the money, only the letter saying for me to come." Her voice shook but she forced her gaze to meet Sloan's. It was the truth, and she mentally dared him to deny it.

"He sent the money." All eyes turned to Maggie. She stepped forward. "I helped him write the letter, and I put the money inside the envelope."

Julianne felt faint. There had been no money with the letter. Had her uncle known about the letters? Had *he* taken the money? She felt Maggie's accusing gaze upon her and lifted her head. "I never received the money. I promise, Maggie."

"Then where is it?" Sloan barked.

Unable to hold them at bay any longer, tears filled her eyes as she pleaded with Maggie and Sloan. "You have to believe me. I never got the money. When Mr. Kellywood didn't send it, I signed on with Mr. Mercer."

"Look, you owe me money. That's all there is to it." Sloan took a threatening step toward her once again. "And I want it now." He snarled the words through clenched teeth.

"Sloan." The warning came from the lumber boss. "Touch the woman again, and I'll remove you from my camp."

"I don't have it," Julianne whispered, brokenhearted. "I don't have fifty cents to my name. I can't pay you back money I don't have." She'd spent her last dime on the last four days at the boarding house and the little bit of food she'd eaten. She trembled with fear. Would the lumber boss have her removed from camp, too? The thought of going back to Seattle and once again being ogled by the men there made her want to curl up and die. And traveling all the way back to New York was out of the question.

The sickening smell of body odor intensified as an old grizzled-looking man stepped up beside her. Brown spittle covered his gray beard. "I said I'll pay you one hundred dollars. Let me have the girlie, Sloan."

The thought of being bought by the smelly man was almost more than Julianne could take. Given a choice, she'd go back to town and face the men there. Surely there were a few civilized males in Seattle who would protect her. Julianne squeezed her eyes shut. *Lord, please don't let this happen*, she silently pleaded.

The man's renewed bid started the bargaining again and the crowd surged forward as each man tried to outbid the others. Her eyes snapped open, and she searched for a way out of the crowd. Julianne felt herself being pressed against the big logger boss.

He reached out and steadied her. "Ain't nobody going to buy the little lady today, and that's final." At the men's loud complaining, he said, "Tomorrow is Sunday. We'll have a contest then. Whoever wins the contest will win the right to pay this little lady's debt. Until then, no one so much as lays a hand on her, you hear? I expect you men to get back to work. We have logs to cut." With that he stomped off.

Julianne watched the men slowly follow the lumber boss. She took a deep breath of clean mountain air and silently prayed again. *Thank You, Lord*.

Maggie came up to Julianne. "Well, I guess you and I are stuck with each other until after the contest." Julianne felt a tear slide slowly down her cheek and saw Maggie's look of disgust. "Now don't go getting soft on me. Let's go fix supper for these men, and maybe we'll think of a way for you to get out of this mess."

Julianne heard Maggie murmur as she headed toward the cookshack, "Wish I'd left her by the river."

Caleb Hansen watched from the edge of the woods. He'd witnessed the whole sorry event as it unfolded. Evidently, he wasn't the only one with problems. The young woman looked and acted innocent of any wrong-doing, but he'd met many a woman who could look and act innocent.

The baby in his arms whimpered. "What am I going to do about you?" he asked the little fellow. Terrible regrets assailed him and grief weighed heavy on his heart. He'd had great plans for the sister he'd not seen in years. Those plans now lay in a grave on the edge of his property and he was left to raise her infant son alone.

The swell of pain that filled his chest was beyond tears. His throat felt raw with unuttered protests. Why had he been robbed of the only person he held dear? Why must this precious baby boy grow up without a mother? Why did she have to die? Why, why, why?

Holding his jaw rigid against the pain that made him want to crumble, Caleb made his way down the steep incline to the cookshack. He couldn't afford to be distracted by grief. But reality had stared him in the face the last couple of mornings, and he found himself struggling for courage, strength and determination to carry out the task the Lord had seen fit to place upon him.

For now, he'd have to ask Maggie to watch the little tyke so Caleb could help fell trees today. Due to the commotion the foreman had needed to settle a few minutes ago, they had lost valuable sunlight. They would need every able-bodied man to make up the time. And in the logging business time was money.

The savory smell of stew and cornbread permeated the cookshack. Julianne watched the baby sleeping as Maggie stirred pots of meat and potatoes and checked her bread in the oven. Several cakes of corn pone already cooled on the long plank that served as a table.

The baby's little lips twitched into what appeared to be a smile. "He's such a sweet little fellow. Why is his mama not tending to him today?" Julianne smiled down into the baby's sleeping face.

"Ain't none of our business. If Caleb had wanted us to know, he'd a told us." Maggie dropped another pan of cornbread on the makeshift table. "Besides, we got other problems to think about."

Julianne's heart went out to the little one sleeping so contentedly as if he hadn't a care in the world. That would all change soon enough.

Her parents had died when she was eight years old and left her in the care of her mother's only sister and her husband. But her aunt was no match for her bullying husband and Julianne had felt his wrath constantly. His ambition to belong to the elite of New York's growing city kept him overworked and dissatisfied with those in his household. They'd had to perform and entertain at his whim, and heaven forbid they have lives of their own. Fear shivered down her spine and she clamped her lips even tighter. She wouldn't even *think* his name.

"Can you wash clothes?"

Maggie's question pulled her from her troubled thoughts. She looked up into the older woman's tired face. "Of course I can."

"Good. Maybe you could wash the men's clothing for a price, and then pay Sloan back the money you owe him." She stirred the first big pot of stew then moved on to the next.

Powerful relief filled Julianne's heart as a glimmer of hope took root. "Maybe I can. Then I wouldn't become anyone's property."

Maggie laughed. "That is the idea."

"But where would I live? I'd need a place to stay and supplies to wash the clothes." She chewed on the tip of her fingernail. "Do you think the store would give me credit?" Julianne got to her feet and began pacing.

"You're welcome to stay with me, but you'll have to sleep outside on the porch. There's not enough room in my shack for a tick, much less a dog," Maggie offered, pulling down bowls and plates for the men.

The analogy was not lost on Julianne. And the thought of sleeping out on the porch with those men lurking about wasn't something she planned on entertaining, either. She'd worry about where she'd stay later. Right now she had to think about a way to make some money. "I'll need a wash tub and a scrub board and some soap."

Maggie hesitated. "I'm not so sure about credit. We'd have to ask Mr. Miller about that."

The baby awoke with a start and let out a weak cry.

Julianne frowned in the baby's direction, but didn't move. The cries grew in force till they seemed like one long scream, which caused Maggie to almost drop a pan of cornbread.

"Pick him up for goodness sake." Maggie ordered, righting the hot pan.

Reluctantly Julianne walked to where the crying baby lay. She leaned toward him and whispered, "Don't get used to this." She slid her hands under his tiny little body, lifting him up to her shoulder. He smelled of baby and milk. She cuddled him close to her heart, swaying back and forth until he settled down.

Maggie glanced at her. "You sure are good with that baby."

"I should be, I used to help my aunt with her children," Julianne muttered, remembering the twin babies she'd practically raised in New York. Day in, day out, she'd bathed, fed and diapered her cousins, falling into bed at night completely exhausted. She'd been nine years old when they were born and she'd cared for them until she fled her uncle's home for Seattle. It had been much too heavy a load and she mourned her stolen youth.

The little guy's eyes began to droop, but every now and then he'd jerk as if afraid he might fall. A tiny spark of empathy stirred in Julianne's heart. She'd had the same feeling ever since she stepped off the ship.

She heard laughter and raucous voices outside. Maggie rushed to the side door and shushed the men as they stomped wood shavings off their boots and came in from their hard day's work. They cast furtive glances Julianne's way, the braver ones studying her with curious intensity. Each man accepted a bowl of stew and a generous hunk of cornbread from Maggie and made his way to a table.

Julianne felt uncomfortable under their stares. They

talked in soft whispers as they ate, their eyes darting back and forth between Julianne and their plates.

As if the baby sensed her unease, he began to fret. Stiffening his little body, a single cry of protest escaped. Maggie thrust a bottle with a sticky rubber nipple into her hands and shoved her toward the back door.

Julianne walked outside and sank down on the back step. The baby snuggled against her as he drank from the bottle. He was such a tiny little thing. He couldn't be more than a few days old. Helpless in the situation life had placed him. Same as Julianne.

She brushed the fine blond hair across his forehead. Deep blue eyes stared up at her as he drank. Julianne remembered a woman aboard the ship she'd traveled on. She'd had blond hair and soft blue eyes, and had been pregnant. Had she been Caleb's wife, and was this their child?

"We'll make it, little fellow. Just you wait and see." She whispered the words of encouragement with a slight smile of defiance. They weren't beaten yet.

"He seems to like you."

Startled by the voice, Julianne glanced uneasily over her shoulder.

A man stepped out of the shadows.

"I didn't mean to scare you." He offered, easing down to sit beside her on the wooden step. Julianne eyed him nervously. She'd learned quickly not to trust any man, even if he did have a pleasant look, nice smile and soft voice.

She didn't know what to say, so she said nothing. The only sound in the evening air was the mewing sound the baby made as he ate. She sought a topic of conversion to fill the silence but found nothing of interest. Only her problems were uppermost in her mind.

"He's a greedy little fella, isn't he?" The man leaned forward and touched the baby's soft cheek.

Expecting the offensive odor of sweat, Julianne was instead surprised by the clean scent of lye soap.

Earlier in the day, when he had brought the baby in and passed him off to Maggie, Julianne had been so wrapped up in her own troubles that she hadn't paid much attention to the man. So this was Caleb. The Caleb Maggie seemed to think so highly of.

Now, sitting just inches away from the man, she took the time to get a better look at him. Light brown hair touched his collar. It curled on the ends, making her wonder if it was as soft as it looked. His profile was sharp and confident, his skin bronzed by the wind and sun. His firm mouth tilted upward slightly as if always on the edge of a smile. The fingers that stroked the baby's cheek were callused, tapered and strong.

But the thing that drew her attention most was his eyes. They looked moist as he studied the baby in her arms. They were an unusual shade of green, polished jade, and she detected a touch of sorrow in their depths. As if too much heartbreak had entered his life.

Again she wondered about the baby's mother.

As if he could read her mind, Caleb answered. "His mother is dead. I buried her the day the ship arrived in port. She didn't even have time to name him."

Julianne heard the heartache in his voice and felt the urge to comfort him. "I'm sorry," was all she could get out of her tight throat.

"Maggie tells me your name is Julianne. I'm Caleb Hansen." He raised his head and studied her face. Julianne wondered what he saw. She knew she was no beauty. Her uncle had told her she had hair the color of coal and that her lips were too big for her face.

Not that it mattered; the last thing she wanted was for a man with a baby to find her attractive. The baby squirmed as if in protest to her thoughts. She gently transferred him into Caleb's arms.

Caleb put a cloth over his shoulder and rested the baby against it. He gently patted the little fellow on the back until a loud burp reached their ears. When Caleb eased the infant from his shoulder, a small dribble of milk escaped the corner of the baby's mouth. She watched him wipe the edge of the tiny lips with tender care that seemed impossible with those large hands.

Settling the child in the crook of his arm, he stood. "Thank you for watching him."

For reasons she didn't understand, Julianne didn't want Caleb to go. "Have you eaten?" He mounted the horse with the baby in one arm, emphasizing the strength of his thighs and powerful, well-muscled arms.

"Not yet, but I'm heading home. I've got food at the cabin. Thanks again for taking care of the little one." He turned the horse to go.

Julianne watched Caleb and the baby until she could no longer see them through the trees. Then she turned wearily to help Maggie with the massive cleanup of the kitchen. She tried to maintain a positive outlook, but to-morrow loomed like a giant thundercloud, much like the ones hovering over the sawmill camp right now. In fact, in the four days since she'd arrived she'd only caught an occasional glimpse of the sun. That sat slightly at odds with her nature. Lord knew, she needed all the positive reinforcement she could get and a little sunshine would go a long way.

Chapter 2

The next morning, Caleb tramped through the logging camp. Young and old men alike practiced for the upcoming contest. He stopped beside the man who had started the whole mess.

Sloan glanced over at him and gave a brief nod. "Did you come to compete too, Hansen?" His gaze moved to Julianne. "If I'd known how beautiful she was, I might not have married Susan."

The foreman joined the two men. "You could put a stop to this now, Sloan. I could change the prize to a day off with pay and the men wouldn't argue too much."

"She owes me." Sloan spat on the ground and stomped away.

Caleb watched him leave. What caused a man to turn so bitter? He pulled his attention from the young man and nodded hello to the foreman. "You going to join the competition, boss?"

"Nah, I have to keep everyone in line."

Caleb had found William Taylor to be a man of honor and a fair and generous boss. And he ruled his loggers with a sternness that not many men dared to defy.

"How about you?" Taylor asked. "You going to compete?"

"I'm not sure." Caleb had asked himself the same question last night. The baby needed someone to take care of him. Caleb knew he could not stay up all night with a crying baby and work the next day. The way the little one stiffened and drew his tiny legs up against his chest worried Caleb. A woman seemed to instinctively know about these things but he was at a loss.

His cabin might not be the fanciest but it was one of the nicest around. Roomy with a loft and a modern wood cookstove. Julianne would have a home if she so chose.

Caleb refused to explore the unfamiliar emotions he felt every time he saw the black-haired beauty, but long after darkness had settled over the evening before, he'd remembered her beautiful, clear blue eyes and the determined expression on her face as she'd stood her ground with Sloan.

Now both men looked straight ahead. The foreman focused on the trees that would be felled that day. Caleb's attention focused solely on Julianne.

He watched Maggie come up and place the baby in Julianne's arms. A frown marred her pretty features as she looked down at the infant. He wondered at the cause. Didn't she like babies? He thought all women had a built in love for a motherless child, yet that definitely was not motherly love on her face.

Questions swirled through his mind. Had she taken the money as she was accused of doing? Could she be trusted to watch the baby? Which brought up another question: Exactly what did he know about her?

Absolutely nothing.

"If you compete, there isn't another man around here that could beat you. That baby needs a mother, and the woman needs a place to stay. It would be a good trade-off for both of you." The foreman walked away before Caleb could protest or comment.

He continued to stroll through the camp. Pieces of conversations met his ears. Each man boasted about what would become of the lovely Miss Julianne once he won the contest.

"I'll have her baking a cake before sundown, if I win," Ben bragged as he flung his ax at a tree stump.

His buddy laughed. "Yeah, me too, but after that, she could get started on my washing. I've worn these clothes for over a week."

Caleb moved on, fighting the urge to smash both men in the mouth for their lack of consideration. As he passed Marcus Harvey and another logger, he heard Marcus crow.

"She's a pretty little thing. I'm looking forward to making her pay for that fare she stole." Marcus was a big burly man who enjoyed acting like a tough guy. Rumor had it he'd killed a man, but it was only hearsay and had never been proven.

Caleb winced at the thought of Julianne or any woman at the mercy of Marcus Harvey. Finally, he wound up where Julianne stood. "How's the baby?"

He watched her blue eyes widen with surprise, though she tried hard to hide it. He'd evidently startled her again. He was intrigued by the mystery that surrounded the woman in front of him.

"He's fine. I was wondering if you've thought of a name for him, yet." She smoothed the hair off the baby's face and rocked from side to side.

Caleb wondered if she rocked to sooth her own nerves or the child's. "Not yet, I'm thinking along the lines of Jonathan. What do you think?"

"Jonathan." The name came out a whisper as if she were testing its flavor against her tongue. "It means Jehovah's gift." She squinted up at him. "You should consider him a gift from the Lord. I like it. It sounds strong. A man needs a strong name."

The question was out before he could stop it. "How did you get into this predicament, Julianne?" He watched her eyes take on a faraway look.

Bitterness laced her next words. "I trusted the wrong man."

Screams of frustration longed to escape Julianne's throat as she watched her future being decided for her. She felt frozen in limbo where all decisions and actions evaded her.

Strange and disquieting thoughts had plagued her all through the night, not to mention the straw tick she'd slept on, on Maggie's floor. She'd awakened this morning sick with the struggle inside.

Now, as she observed the two leaders of the competition, a small glimmer of hope helped her raise her chin and muster all the dignity she could.

Caleb and one other man were in the lead. In the ax throwing, both men had hit the bull's-eye on the target. Caleb had climbed and cut the top off of a tree faster than anyone else. The other man, named Marcus, had split more wood than Caleb. He'd only won by one log but he'd still won. And now it looked as if Caleb was using all the strength he had to fell a tree before Marcus.

She admired the way the muscles in his back and shoulders bulged, as he dragged the saw back and forth against the tree. Rivulets of sweat ran down his face and into his eyes. Still, he continued to bunch his muscles and work faster.

The thought of Caleb Hansen winning the race wasn't too distasteful. The other men respected him, and it appeared most of them wanted him to win. The few brief times she'd seen him, he'd said little, the semblance of a quiet man. But her aunt had said it was the quiet ones you had to beware of. Of course, her aunt had been talking about Julianne, not a man, so should that be a characteristic by which she judged Caleb?

She chose to believe he was the kind of man who would pay off her debt and then allow her to pay him back as she got the money.

Her gaze moved to Marcus. Now, here was trouble in capital letters. A burly man with arms as big around as some of the trees that surrounded the camp, he had a mean attitude and cursing came as easily as breathing. She shuddered to think what kind of man he was. She doubted he would be willing to wait for her to repay him. But she had news for him. He'd have to.

"If you're a praying woman, you better pray that one doesn't win." Maggie spoke in a low, warning voice, as if afraid that Marcus would hear. She held the baby against her shoulder and patted his back. She used her chin to point at Marcus.

Julianne tore her gaze away from the men. "Why?" She struggled to make her voice nonchalant. "It really doesn't matter to me who wins. I'll make an arrangement with the winner, he'll pay Sloan and I'll pay him back with the money I make from taking in laundry."

Maggie shook her head. "Honey, not to embarrass you, but these men have been without a woman for a long time. Do you really think they will just give Sloan the money, and then wait for you to pay it back?" She rocked the sleeping baby.

"You don't mean…?" Julianne's hand went to her mouth.

The older woman leaned closer and whispered. "Marcus is a mean one. He will demand full payment of his money from you, and he's not afraid to take it out of your hide. If you know what I mean." Maggie pulled away to cheer on Caleb. "Keep at it Caleb, he's almost whupped!" She bellowed with the rest of the crowd. The baby uttered a sharp cry of protest as if he, too, were against Marcus winning.

Julianne looked at the man they had been discussing. He stood at least a head and a half taller than she. He caught her eye for a moment and grinned, but his eyes remained flat, hard and passionless. It frightened her to think what he had in store for her.

After quieting the baby, Maggie leaned close again. "Now Caleb, there is a fine young man. He's got his reason for wanting to win too, though." She paused. "He needs a mama for this little boy of his. I imagine he figures you will fit the bill."

"No." Julianne whispered. That was one of the reasons she'd run from New York—to get away from screaming children and adults who tried to run her life. She couldn't believe this was happening.

"Oh, being married to Caleb wouldn't be so bad. He's

got a real nice cabin built off in the woods, and he's a Bible-reading man."

Bible reading or not, Julianne wanted no part of taking care of someone else's child. And she knew that reading the Bible didn't necessarily make anyone a better man. Her uncle read the good book every night. What good had it done? Not one whit. He still beat her and turned her into the house slave.

But it hadn't always been like that. She had earlier memories of an uncle who had been kind and patient. He'd bought her a pony and taught her to ride.

"Timber!" The shout came from Caleb.

Marcus added his voice to it. "Timber!"

Everyone held their breaths as the mighty pine trees fell in unison.

"I won!" Marcus yelled, jerking his hat off his head and rushing to Julianne.

Before she had a chance to protest, he threw her over his shoulder and started stomping off toward the woods. The pins in her hair fell out with each pounding step he took. The smell of sweat and body odor assaulted her senses and made her stomach queasy.

Marcus came to a bone-jarring halt. "Get out of my way, Hansen. I won fair and square."

Julianne tried to pull herself upright but the big man slapped her on her bottom. The sound echoed in the silent camp. Mortified, Julianne's embarrassment turned to hot, burning anger. She turned her head to the side and sank her teeth into the soft skin above Marcus's belt.

Marcus dumped Julianne at his feet then drew his arm back to hit her.

"I wouldn't hit her if I were you, Harvey." Caleb's warning rang out before the slap connected.

"Who's gonna stop me? You?" He grabbed Julianne by the hair and jerked her head back.

Her cry of pain tore at Caleb's insides. He took a step forward. His gaze locked with hers, and he witnessed the fear, pain and humiliation on her soft features. Marcus pulled a knife from his boot and pressed it into her throat in one liquid motion. "Hold it right there, Hansen."

Caleb stopped. A small stream of blood traveled from the tip of the knife, down her throat and into the material at her neck. He didn't move, he didn't breathe, he simply held her gaze and silently begged her to trust him.

He held his hands up. "Now what?"

Marcus looked around the logging camp. Men watched his every move. It was apparent he hadn't planned on revealing the knife, but pride made him bluster through the threat. Twisting his hand in her hair and pushing the knife a little harder against her throat, he jerked Julianne to her feet. He saw the foreman standing off to one side with his hands behind his back. "Me and the little gal are gonna go settle up."

Caleb stepped closer. "I don't think so, Harvey. You're either going to let her go or kill her now." He made eye contact with the foreman.

Julianne gave a tiny squeak as the knife cut deeper.

The foreman stepped forward. "Marcus, I'm not so sure you won. The trees fell about the same time and me and the boys here will be the judge of who won."

Marcus focused on the foreman and shook his head. "No, sir. I won." He lightened the pressure on Julianne's neck.

It was all the distraction Caleb needed. He rushed at Marcus, grabbed the hand that held the knife and forced it away from Julianne.

The camp went wild. Marcus kicked Julianne away

from him and she fell, her head hitting a tree, her limp body unmoving.

In a matter of seconds, Caleb had Marcus on the ground, his feet and hands bound with rope.

Caleb rushed to Julianne. Blood caked her throat and the front of her dress. He scooped up her unconscious form. "Maggie!"

"I'm right here. You don't have to shout." She scolded him. "Take her into the cookshack."

The baby slept soundly in Maggie's arms, unaware that there had been a fight and someone had just faced the jowls of death and survived.

Caleb laid Julianne down on the kitchen floor. "Do you think she's going to be all right, Maggie?" Her eyelashes looked like black soot against her colorless face.

Maggie started to hand him the sleeping baby. "Here take care of your son, while I tend to her."

"My son?"

Maggie heaved a breath. "Yes, Caleb. Take the baby." She knelt beside Julianne's still form as he tucked the baby into the crook of his arm.

"Maggie, he's not my…"

"Stop yer yammering, Caleb, and let me see to this child."

The impatience in Maggie's voice halted his shocked denial that Jonathan was his son. How on earth could she think this was his son? He saw Maggie at least once a week and he'd never carried a baby into her place until three days ago when he'd stopped by and asked her what to feed him. The place had been full and Maggie had rushed around serving everyone but still had taken time to answer his questions. Oh well, it was just one more thing he'd have to settle later.

He turned to go find Marcus Harvey. With each step his anger grew. How could any man hurt a woman like that? He'd seen the pleasure in Marcus's eyes every time he pressed the knife blade deeper into her soft creamy throat.

He came to the spot where he'd left the logger. Several men stood around smoking and talking in low voices. "Where is he?" Caleb asked.

"The foreman took him," Ben Wheeler said.

Caleb turned to the small man with wire-framed glasses. "Where'd he take him to?" He shifted the baby to his other arm.

"He didn't say and we didn't ask. Just loaded him in the wagon and took him out of here."

Caleb thought about following them. The deep ruts of the wagon would be easy enough to follow. At that moment, the baby stretched and warm moisture coated Caleb's arm. He looked down at the tiny red face as the baby strained, his arms flailing, and the diaper became heavier. Jonathan thrashed his legs and Caleb knew from experience that if the diaper wasn't changed in the next few moments, things would get ugly. First things would have to come first.

Sloan stood off to the side, "I want my money, Hansen."

Caleb dug in his pocket and pulled out a hundred dollars. "There, that's all you're getting. Stay away from Julianne." He waited for Sloan's stoic nod, and then hurried back to the cookshack.

Chapter 3

Julianne woke slowly. Her cheek burned, and her head hurt. She reached up to touch her throbbing neck.

"Don't be messing with my handiwork," Maggie scolded gently. She caught Julianne's fingers before they could touch the material at her neck. "It's just a scratch."

The recent nightmare flooded in on her. She sat up. "Where is he?" The cry tore from her raw throat.

Maggie put a hand on her shoulder. "He's not going to hurt you anymore, Julianne. Caleb and the lumber boss made sure of it."

Julianne pushed her hair out of her face. "They did?"

The older woman nodded, "They did."

Caleb came through the side door, Jonathan screaming in his arms. "I'm sorry, Maggie. He's wet, and I have to get his things."

"That's okay. She's awake now." Maggie got up and went to a saddlebag that sat in a corner.

Julianne watched Caleb jiggle the baby while he waited. She knew she owed him her life. A new fear entered her heart. How much would he demand for payment?

"Here, I'll take him." Maggie took the crying baby and moved to one of the side tables to change his diaper.

"Feeling any better?" Caleb asked. He squatted down beside Julianne.

She nodded.

"He won't bother you again, I promise." He raised his hand to touch the white cloth that bound her neck, and then dropped it to his side.

"Thank you." Julianne felt his gaze sweep over her face. Whatever words she would have added vanished with his appraisal.

Caleb rose to his feet and extended his hand to help her up. "Do you feel like taking a walk with me? Or would you rather stay here and talk?"

Julianne studied the tanned, callused hand. It was large and full of strength, much like his broad shoulders. Would he hurt her, too? She raised her gaze to his face and sought the answers to her question in his eyes. He had an air of calm that comforted her.

"Trust me, Julianne. I promise I will never hurt you." Caleb continued to hold out his hand.

Julianne placed hers in his. He'd protected her before; she had to trust he meant what he said. "I think I'd like some fresh air."

He turned to Maggie with a questioning gaze.

"You two go on. I'll take care of this little boy." Maggie held a bottle to Jonathan's mouth.

Caleb led Julianne out the side door and into a grove of trees. They walked a bit, Julianne focusing on the dirt tracks beneath her feet. They were smooth as glass and it was obvious something heavy moved across them regularly, but the tracks were not the same as those that carriage or buggy wheels made.

Curiosity got the better of her. "What are these tracks called?"

"They're skid tracks. We use metal skids to haul the timber over to the sawmill. Folks round here call this Skid Road." They continued walking until they came to a small clearing. Pink, purple and white flowers grew all around them. Julianne sat down on a large stump. She took a deep breath, inhaling the fresh clear air as she waited for Caleb to speak.

"We need each other," he blurted.

Julianne didn't need him. She didn't need anyone. And she definitely didn't need a baby.

You needed him a few minutes ago, her inner voice reminded her. She decided to do the polite thing and hear him out. When he finished, she would explain to him that she was willing to reimburse him for paying off Sloan, and then she'd go back to Seattle and find a place to live. The thought that she had no money to pay for a home tugged at her exhausted mind, but she ignored it.

When she didn't argue, Caleb continued. "You need someone to protect you, and I need a mother for Jonathan."

He knelt down in front of her. "Julianne, I will make you a good husband."

Husband? Who said anything about him becoming her husband? All he competed for was to pay off her debt to Sloan. What was it with men? First Marcus had thought he owned her, and now so did Caleb.

"I don't want nor do I need a husband, Mr. Hansen." She looked into his green eyes. "I'll pay you back, if you will pay Sloan off for me, but I'm not going to marry you." She watched the soft eyes turn to hard emeralds.

He stood to his feet and looked down on her. "Didn't you come here to marry Sloan?"

"Yes, but I was…"

Caleb cut off her words. "What? Were you or were you not going to marry him when you got here?"

Julianne jumped to her feet at the anger in his voice. Could she make it back to the cookshack before he lost his temper and did who knows what? "That doesn't matter now. He's already married." She stood her ground even though her brain told her to flee.

He tilted his head to the side. "Are you afraid of me, Julianne?"

She knew he'd seen her fear. What should she say? Yes, all men scare me? Or deny the truth?

"A little."

Caleb watched her bottom lip quiver. He didn't enjoy seeing fear in the eyes of any woman. Towering over someone only made that person feel more threatened. He sat down on the grass in front of her and stretched his legs out in front of him. "I'm sorry. I won't hurt you." He prayed his actions convinced her that his words were true.

Julianne cautiously sat back down on the stump. "It's not your fault. I…" Her voice trailed away, and she bit her bottom lip.

"It's okay, Julianne. The last two days have been hard on you."

He watched her swipe at her eyes as she nodded her head. His stomach clenched, and he wondered how she would take his suggestion. If she was this afraid of him now, what might she say when she heard him out?

"Julianne, if you don't marry me then you need to prepare yourself for the reaction of the men. There are more men in these parts like Marcus. Unfortunately, this land and the men in it aren't tame. They are a rough bunch looking for female companionship and not necessarily the marrying kind." He stopped to let his words seep in.

Lord please let her understand I'm trying to help her, not scare her.

He stared intently at her face, willing her to accept the truth of his words. Her skin appeared transparent. Caleb wondered if it was from the knife wound or if his words had further terrified her.

"You could always return home."

"I can't."

The raw sounding whisper tore at his heart.

"If it's money, I'll help you." It would take all the money he had saved, but he'd rather see her home safe than in Washington where things were still too rough for a single woman, especially a frightened single woman.

Her tear-filled eyes met his. "No, I can never go back," she whispered, as if afraid her thoughts might turn to reality if she said them aloud. She seemed to fight some inner battle before she straightened her shoulders and looked him square in the eyes. "I'll marry you."

Caleb stood to his feet. "Are you sure?" He took both her hands in his. *Why can't she go back? What has she done?* Again, the thought occurred to him that he knew nothing about the woman in front of him. Yet, he felt the need to protect her from her present as well as her past.

"Julianne, whatever you are running from will probably find you."

Her head snapped up and her mouth shot open.

Caleb witnessed wild terror fill her eyes. "With that in mind, do you still want to marry me?"

His gaze followed the line of her throat. He saw her swallow hard.

"More than ever."

"How about today?" He searched her sapphire-blue gaze.

"Do you think we can today?" Again her voice was barely above a whisper.

"I'm pretty sure the preacher is still in town." At her quizzical look he explained. "Some of the Mercer brides who came in on the ship with you planned on getting married today." He could have kicked himself at the hurt look she shot him from under soot-colored lashes.

He gently squeezed her hands. "I'm sorry. It seems I keep saying the wrong thing, doesn't it?"

He watched her lips tremble in a watery smile and she squared her shoulders bravely before answering. "I guess we'd better get the baby and go to the church."

Caleb admired her quick decision-making. She was a game little thing. Approval warmed his insides.

"We don't have to take Jonathan with us, if you don't want to. I'm sure Maggie won't mind watching him for us."

Julianne pulled her hands from his and settled her shawl more securely about her shoulders then looked at him.

"Mr. Hansen, if we are going to become a family, we might as well start acting like one now."

He walked beside her. "In that case, Julianne, maybe you should call me Caleb."

She followed him back to camp, masking her inner turmoil with a deceptive calmness. A faint thread of hysteria threatened to overwhelm her. She wanted to scream and beat her fists against his wide shoulders at the injustice of it all. She hadn't even had time to think through each decision. It was a matter of do this, or else. What kind of choice was that?

He seemed very alert to the woods around them and Julianne wondered if he was as worried about Marcus as she was.

He could protect her from bullies like Marcus. But what kind of life would she have without love? When she'd escaped New York, she'd thought there would be the opportunity to fall in love with her new husband—the very thing she craved more than anything else in the world. Sloan's letters had promised that he would love her. How she'd been fooled!

She looked at Caleb. He'd never promised to love her. He just needed a mother for his baby. Her throat ached with defeat.

"So you two are back." Maggie stood in the small clearing by the kitchen, holding Jonathan in her arms. "I hope you've come to your senses and decided to marry each other."

Julianne watched Caleb take his son and cuddle him in his big arms. His eyes gentled as he looked down on the baby.

"We have. Can you gather up his things, Maggie?

Maggie let out a whoop. "I'll keep the baby. You two go on." She reached for Jonathan.

"No!" both Julianne and Caleb stated at the same time.

The baby let out a squall, and Caleb pressed him to his chest and jiggled him up and down.

Julianne wondered why Caleb didn't want to leave the baby with Maggie. Moments earlier, he'd offered to. Her gaze moved to the man who would soon be her husband. His voice was low, reminding her of warm honey as he soothed the infant.

Jonathan settled against Caleb's shoulder. In the same soothing voice he told Maggie, "We decided to take Jonathan with us. We'll feel more like a family."

"Won't help much with the honeymoon," Maggie grumbled.

Julianne felt an unwelcome blush creep into her cheeks. She averted her gaze from him, humiliatingly conscious of Caleb's scrutiny, and studied the mass of trees to her right. Would he expect her to perform her wifely duties tonight?

"Here's his bag and a fresh blanket, but I really think it's too soon to take this little one on a trip." Julianne turned just in time to have the baby's things thrust into her arms.

Caleb laughed. "It's only an hour's ride, Maggie. I'm certain he'll be fine. We'll have a late lunch at the wharf and make it home by dark." He pushed back the blond hair that fell across his forehead. The tensing of his jaw betrayed his deep frustration. So, Julianne permitted herself a quiet assurance. *He's nervous, too.*

Maggie moved to his side and kissed the baby on the cheek. She turned around and crossed her arms with a stern look directed toward Julianne. "Have you truly ever watched a baby by yourself?"

Julianne pulled her shoulders back and held her head high. "As a matter of fact, I have. I have five cousins, and two of those are twins. The twins were newborns when I started taking care of them."

Caleb draped his right arm around Maggie's shoulder and gave her a little hug. "We'll do fine, Maggie. Can we borrow the supply wagon?"

Her wrinkled face melted into smiles of pleasure. "Yeah, take the wagon."

He leaned down and kissed her on the cheek. "Thank you, Maggie. I'll take good care of it."

She playfully slapped him away. "Stop that, you're almost a married man."

Julianne watched the exchange with an odd twinge of envy.

Caleb handed her the baby. "I'm going to hook up the wagon. I'll be right back for you and the little one."

His gaze searched her face. She wasn't sure what he looked for or what he saw. Was he seeking reassurance that they were doing the right thing? Did he care about what she might feel? Was he worried she would be a bad wife? Were the same warning voices whispering in his head?

He nodded, as if coming to a decision then strode away. "He's a good man, Julianne. You'll see." Maggie touched the baby's head one last time then returned to the cookshack.

Julianne prayed Maggie was right.

She took a deep breath and gathered the baby closer. Soon she would be Mrs. Caleb Hansen and this little guy's mother. Deep in her heart, Julianne knew that when she took those vows they would be bonded for life.

She pushed the fear of the future to the back of her mind. She held her head high, picked up her skirts and went in search of Caleb.

Chapter 4

Julianne still couldn't believe she was Mrs. Caleb Hansen. The preacher had pronounced his blessing on them, along with six other couples, on the tiny porch of the boarding house. She had not enjoyed her stay here earlier in the week, had enjoyed even less the blatant stares of the men. She could hardly wait till they left the Puget Sound area behind.

She looked down at the little ring that circled the finger on her left hand. A heart rested in the center surrounded by vines. It was simple in design and yet it was the most beautiful piece of jewelry she'd ever owned. Ever seen, for that matter.

She finished changing Jonathan's diaper. The baby cooed at her and she gently picked him up. "Well, it looks like you and I are a family." He grabbed a strand of her hair and gave it a tug.

Untangling his fingers, she made her way back to

Caleb and the wagon. "We're ready now." She watched as he took the baby's things and placed them under the seat of the wagon.

"Good, we'll get to the cabin a little before nightfall." Caleb turned and helped her up.

Shades of green turned the forest into an enchanting wonderland. The sound of various birdcalls and the creaking of the wagon filled the stillness. Julianne smiled and concentrated on the beautiful scenery around her.

They passed beneath a canopy of branches. She felt safe and protected within its shade. For the first time since she'd arrived, she really enjoyed the sea of green that surrounded her.

"I hope you will be comfortable in the cabin. It's isolated, and you'll be spending your days alone. Or I could take you and Jonathan to camp with me each morning. You could spend time with Maggie."

She kept her gaze trained on his strong hands. They guided the team with gentle strength. "Thanks, I'd like to try a few days alone. I'll enjoy the quiet."

When they finally arrived at her new home, Julianne gasped in surprise as Caleb guided the wagon out into a wide, clear area. They passed a plowed garden that was fenced in with peeled posts and some sort of wire. The dirt looked freshly turned over and she wondered if anything had been planted yet, or if it was still too early. When she left New York there had still been snow on the ground. She loved a garden and that was one thing she knew for certain she could help with.

Caleb's cabin sat in the center of the clearing. The bottom floor looked about two rooms wide, and one room sat above it with two dormers. The new logs gleamed, promising warmth and security. Something Julianne welcomed.

Caleb pulled the wagon to a stop and jumped down. "Here, hand me the baby."

Julianne did as he asked, then began to climb down. She felt his hand on the small of her back. When she turned around her eyes met his. In their depths was an expression she didn't quite recognize. It quickened her heartbeat.

"Welcome to your new home." His warm voice pulled her from the confusion of her heart.

"If you'll take him, I'll put the horses and wagon away. Maggie will have my head if I let them come to harm." Caleb placed the baby gently in her arms then took Jonathan's things and her bag from the wagon and handed them to her.

"Thank you." She put the bags on the ground and tucked the blanket more securely around the baby. Satisfied he was safe from the cool breeze, she reached down and retrieved her things. All she needed was a sick baby on her hands. She took a deep breath, suddenly feeling ill equipped for the task ahead of her.

Caleb touched Jonathan's head and looked into Julianne's eyes. "I hope you will be happy here, Julianne."

She searched his face. What did he expect from her? Whatever it was, she hoped she could provide it. Should she tell him that her misgivings increased by the minute? He held her gaze steadily, expectant it appeared. No, she couldn't trouble him with her own uneasiness. "I'll try to be." To her dismay her voice wavered.

His hand dropped from the baby's head as she turned toward the cabin. She looked over her shoulder as she set the extra things by the door. Caleb was leading the horse to the barn.

Julianne opened the cabin door and stepped inside. Her first impression was one of cleanliness and order. A large table sat in the center of the left side of the room. Toward the back wall was the kitchen.

To her right, opposite the kitchen, a bed covered with a Star of David quilt took up most of the space in that area. A beautifully crafted cradle stood by the side of the bed. Small butterflies and flowers decorated the baby's new bed. At the foot of the bed was a tall wooden divider. One would only have to pull it a few feet to have complete privacy in the bedroom.

She moved to the cradle and laid the baby inside. His sleeping face pouted for a moment before he sighed and stuck his thumb in his mouth. Satisfied he was comfortable, she went back outside to the porch.

She stared at the barn, wondering how long it would be before Caleb would come inside. She picked up her bag and the baby's things and stepped back inside the house. She placed them on the bed then walked to the foot of the stairs. She gripped the post rail, tempted to run up and check whether there was another bedroom or only storage up there.

She heard the scraping of boots against wooden steps and knew the time had come. She wrung her hands together nervously and tiptoed to the baby's side. No help would be forthcoming from the little tyke. His steady breathing told her deep sleep had captured him.

"Anyone home?" Caleb called as he entered the house. He felt out of place in his own house.

She stepped from behind the bedroom divider. "I'm here."

Caleb came further into the room. He pulled out a chair and sank into it, his knees suddenly weak. "I think you and I should talk. Really talk."

He studied her quite openly, watching her inch forward, her bottom lip caught between pearly white teeth. She paused in uncertainty then seemed to gather her courage. Somehow she managed to face him, finely arched eyebrows raised in question. "Okay. What do you want to talk about?"

He motioned to the only other available chair then waited till she was seated. "For starters, we really don't know each other, and we need to. Maybe we should have had this conversation earlier, but since we didn't, I think now would be a good time. Don't you?"

Julianne nodded, but when she didn't say anything, Caleb began to doubt he'd done the right thing by initiating a personal conversation so soon. He should have simply said good-night and gone to bed. Never one to beat the devil around the stump he continued. "I'll start."

Receiving no encouragement from her whatsoever, he began hesitantly. "I'm from New York. I moved here in fifty-nine. I was nineteen years old and green as a gourd." He chuckled softly. "My sister, Estelle, and her husband had just gotten married, and I decided I needed to start a life of my own rather than invade their privacy, them being newlyweds and all." Caleb paused.

"Please go on." Julianne moved forward in her chair.

Finally! Caleb crossed his arms on the table. "I hired on with William Taylor here at the logging camp." He stopped and took a deep breath.

"My sister wrote and told me her husband had been

wounded in the War Between the States. He seemed to recover, although his leg never fully healed. Then infection set in and they had to amputate. He died in November. Estelle was three months pregnant with their first child so I sent the fare for her to come here and live with me. She was supposed to arrive five days ago." His voice broke with huskiness and his eyes stung. "Instead, the captain met me with the news that my sister had died in childbirth aboard his ship just two short days before arriving."

"I'm so sorry, Caleb." Her hand covered his, and then he watched the shock of discovery hit her full force. "Jonathan?"

"Is her son."

Her lip trembled and she closed her eyes for a brief moment. Caleb felt helpless, and for the first time in his life, he was speechless.

"So Jonathan's just seven days old." Her voice sounded vague but he knew that could be deceptive since one expression after another crossed her features. When she looked at him again, her eyes were filled with compassion and something he couldn't quite define. She brushed the back of his hand in a soothing motion. Had she seen the pain of his sister's death in his face? Why had he started this?

"My parents died quite a long time ago, so I know what it's like to grow up without a loving father and mother."

Caleb witnessed her own sorrow deep in her eyes. He turned his hand so that hers rested in his palm. The action seemed to bring her back from the past.

"I'm sorry your sister died but I'm glad she left you baby Jonathan."

"Thank you."

"It's a great responsibility to raise someone else's child. If you have even a small inkling that you can't provide the nurturing and constant attention and love Jonathan needs, then you should place him with a family that can give that type of support."

Her words were an affront to his character, but Caleb suspected she spoke from experience rather than a desire to insult him. He purposefully loaded his answer with double meaning.

"Jonathan is all the family I have left. I already love him and I will protect him with my life. I only want people around him who have his best interests at heart. Less than that is unacceptable." He watched for a change in her composure. Better she should know now what he expected of her.

She smiled. "I'd better get you something to eat."

Surprised again by this unpredictable woman, Caleb tightened his grip on her hand. "I'd rather talk than eat."

Julianne stood to her feet still clutching his hand. "We can do both." She reached out and caught his other hand, pulling him to his feet.

Reluctantly, he let her go but followed close behind. "How about johnnycakes? I have all the fixings."

"Sure, show me where things are, and I'll whip up a batch." She pulled a skillet off one of the hooks that hung over the wood-burning cookstove.

Cornmeal, baking powder, one egg and a jar of milk were soon gathered on the table. "Do you have any sugar?" Julianne found a large wooden bowl and began mixing the ingredients together.

Caleb got the sugar and set it beside the milk. He wondered what she planned on doing with it, but didn't ask.

Jonathan woke up with a cry.

"I'll get him." Caleb picked up the little fellow. He took the baby back into the kitchen where Julianne worked.

"There's a pap feeder in his bag." She offered, pouring batter into a hot skillet. "Be careful, that nipple isn't going to last much longer."

"This was the only thing that arrived with him from the ship." He studied the rubber nipple that fit down over an oval-shaped piece of ceramic bottle. It smelled a little bit and allowed too much milk to flow into the baby's mouth causing a steady dribble out the side and onto Caleb's shirt. He felt pretty sure he could make something a good sight better than this.

The aroma of batter cooking filled the house and caused his stomach to grumble. Julianne worked confidently and quickly. Jonathan sucked noisily on the bottle. If a man didn't know better, he'd be lulled into believing they were a real family.

Almost.

He still didn't know enough about his new wife to trust her. Had she taken Sloan's money? And what was she running from?

She interrupted his thoughts. "Here, give me the baby, and you eat while it's hot."

Caleb did as she said. He watched her sink into a chair and snuggle the baby close. "Aren't you going to eat?"

"As soon as Jonathan finishes." She rocked back and forth with the baby.

He picked up the honey and started to pour it. Her voice stopped him. "Don't you want to try them first?" She brought the baby to her shoulder and gently patted his back.

Caleb tore a bite-size piece of the johnnycake expecting the saltiness of corn pone. Instead, sweetness teased his taste buds. "It's sweet."

"Do you like it?"

Jonathan's burp filled the room and Julianne praised him. "Good boy."

Caleb wondered if Julianne had the same love as he for sweets. "This is very good." Her smile broadened at his words. Well this sure was a blessing. She could cook. It would be worth having a wife just to get a decent meal now and then.

After a few minutes, Jonathan yawned. Caleb stood and reached for the baby. "Here, let me take him. I'll put him to bed." A blush like a shadow ran over her cheeks and she handed the baby to him, her bearing stiff and proud.

"I can do it."

"I'm sure you can, but you need to eat, and I don't mind." Caleb gently took the baby from her. He carried the baby to his cradle and slowly rocked it back and forth until Jonathan fell asleep.

When he returned to the kitchen, Julianne had already cleaned up. She stood by the window looking out into the darkness.

Caleb stopped a few inches from her and looked over her head into the night. If Julianne felt his presence, she didn't show it. The night was black; no light from the moon or the stars could be seen.

"It's late." Her soft whisper surprised him.

Now was the time to bring up the subject he knew both of them had avoided all day. Would she be pleased by his thoughts on the subject? He took a deep breath and blurted.

"It's time for bed, Julianne."

Chapter 5

Julianne spun around and sputtered. "I beg your pardon?"

"That didn't come out right."

She watched Caleb's face and neck turn beet red. "I should say not." New fear enveloped her. Julianne pushed her back as close to the window as she could.

They were married, and he had every right to expect her to sleep with him, but surely there was a better way of saying it. What kind of man had she married? Just when she thought he was kind and understanding, he blurted out "it's time for bed" as if he could demand it.

Caleb took a step away from her. She flinched when he brought one hand up. She expected him to grab her at any moment and drag her to bed.

He combed his fingers through his hair looking even more embarrassed. "Look, I only meant it is time for us to get some sleep. You can take the bed down here, and I'll take the one upstairs."

Her gaze followed his pointing finger. "It was to be my room anyway until I could build a second set of rooms on the back."

He didn't mean to sleep with her? To make her perform her wifely duties? She studied him for several long moments. Could he be believed?

"Look, you and I don't know each other well enough to share that kind of intimacy. I want my wife to be in love before we are man and wife in more than just name. I believe that is the way God would want it to be, also." He dropped his hands. "I moved my stuff up there a few days ago, when I thought my sister would be living here with me."

Julianne wanted to believe him. Even as he climbed the stairs, she still wasn't sure of his intentions.

For several long minutes she heard him moving around above. The creak of a mattress told her he'd lain down. "Good night, Julianne."

She moved to her own bed and sat down. "Good night, Caleb."

A little later, his soft snores filled the house. Julianne checked on the baby and then prepared for bed. She lay on the soft feather mattress listening to her new husband sleep above her.

The baby woke her from restless sleep several times during the night, needing to be changed and fed. Then he spent at least an hour grunting and whimpering as if his tummy hurt. Finally, nearing daybreak, Julianne snuggled him close to her in the bed and he fell asleep, his little body shuddering with sighs. She'd taken care of his needs all while praying he wouldn't wake the man upstairs.

When morning came, Julianne was exhausted. Long before the sun rose in the sky, she heard Caleb get up and move around. His soft footsteps came down the stairs and moved about the kitchen.

She peeked from under the covers to see what he was doing. Julianne sighed, glad he'd found the johnnycakes she'd left out for his breakfast.

Then he turned in her direction. Julianne closed her eyes tightly and pretended to be asleep. She felt his warm lips on her forehead and heard his soft whisper.

"Have a good day, Julianne. Be sure and bolt the door when I leave. Don't go into the woods today, we have a lot to go over before you leave the yard." He kissed her forehead once more and left.

As soon as the door shut, Julianne bolted from the bed and locked the door. She heard his soft chuckle on the other side. Mortified that he hadn't left, she raced back to the bed and dived under the covers.

Then she giggled.

He'd cared enough to make sure she had bolted the door. It was sneaky and sweet at the same time. Her heart warmed toward her new husband.

In a matter of minutes, she was sound asleep.

Jonathan woke her several hours later. Julianne quickly replaced his wet diaper and fed him milk from the leather pouch Caleb kept in the square wooden box that held the butter and cream. Then she ate a johnny-cake from the night before. Next, she prepared a pot of stew and placed it on the stove to cook. She didn't want to admit it, but she was thoroughly enjoying her morning.

She straightened the little cabin and put Jonathan down for a nap. Her gaze moved to the room upstairs. Should she go up and clean it?

Julianne made sure the front door was bolted and then climbed the stairs. A bed took up most of the floor. She noted it hadn't been made and wondered if she should make it. But if she did, he would know she had been in his room, and she wasn't sure she wanted him to know she'd been snooping.

Knocking at the door made her decision for her. Julianne raced down the stairs as fast as her feet would let her without slipping. She crossed to the door and demanded, "Who's there?"

"Maggie."

Julianne unbolted the door. "Come on in." She pulled the door open to its fullest.

Maggie dragged a big bag across the threshold. "It's about time you opened that door. A woman could die of heat stroke while you dallied around in here."

"I'm sorry. I was cleaning and didn't hear you. Besides, it's not hot out there."

Maggie dropped into a chair. "No, but it was a nice trip to make on a sunny day. I'm parched."

Julianne shut the door and turned to face her visitor. "What's in the bag?" Julianne pushed her hair out of her eyes.

"A couple of the men sent their laundry for you to do. You still want to take in laundry, don't you?"

Julianne dipped out a cup of cool well water and gave it to Maggie. "Of course I do, but I'd rather we not tell Caleb just yet."

She watched Maggie tip the cup back and drink its contents before handing it back to her. "Why in the world would you want to keep it a secret from Caleb?"

"Well, he's a proud man, and I feel really bad that he had to pay Sloan the money for my passage. I want to earn the money back and that way we will have it as a nest egg."

Julianne waved the cup. "Would you like more?"

Maggie shook her head. "Naw. I still don't understand what difference it would make if you told Caleb you're doing laundry for the men."

Julianne studied the creases between Maggie's eyes. The woman really didn't understand. "Maggie, if you had a husband, how do you think he would feel if he knew you were cooking for over fifty men a day, three times a day for money?"

She watched as understanding dawned on Maggie. "Are you saying it's an issue of pride?"

Julianne nodded. "That's exactly what I'm saying. After I make enough money to replace what he paid, I'll tell him what I'm doing. Then, if he doesn't want me to continue working, I'll quit."

Maggie slapped the table and laughed. "Okay gal, I'll help you. As far as those mule heads in camp know, I'm doing their laundry and none will be the wiser." She stood to go.

"Thanks, Maggie." Julianne hugged her new friend close. "I promise I'll let Caleb in on our little secret as soon as I can."

The older woman seemed uncomfortable with the hug, but didn't push her away. "Just be sure that you do. I don't like deceiving, Caleb. He's a good man."

Hours later, Caleb wondered what he'd find when he returned home. Would his new wife cower from him? *Lord, please let her learn not to fear me.*

He opened the door a crack. "Is that beef stew I smell?" A quick glance took in the spotless cabin and Julianne standing at the stove with a big ladle in one hand, Jonathan cradled in her other arm.

"It's about ready. Have you washed up?" Julianne stirred the contents of the big pot.

"Sure did. Here, let me take this little fellow off your hands." Caleb walked across the room and took the baby. He sat down in his chair and really looked at the child.

Jonathan had a wide forehead, aqua-colored eyes and a round face. "He looks like Estelle."

Julianne dished up two bowls of stew and set them on the table. "He sure is sweet." She turned to the counter behind her and placed fresh bread on the table.

"That he is." Caleb watched the baby's eyes slowly shut. "I'm going to lay him down, and then we can eat."

He carried the baby into Julianne's bedroom, noticing the neatly made bed and that her things had been put away. A feeling of contentment made him sigh. The baby was well taken care of, the house clean, and dinner smelled delicious. It was what every married man wanted when he came home from a hard day's work.

Caleb returned and took a seat at the table. She surprised him by asking, "Will you say grace, please?"

As he prayed aloud over the meal, he silently prayed for Julianne.

"Lord, thank you for this food and the nourishment for our bodies."

And thank you for Julianne.

"And, bless the hands that have prepared it."

Lord, bless my wife and help her to no longer fear me.

"Keep us safe, in Jesus' name. Amen."

Caleb raised his head and met her clear blue eyes. She smiled, and an expression of satisfaction showed in her eyes. Was she thankful she'd married him? He hoped so.

Julianne fiddled with her ring. "Thank you."

He felt her gaze upon him as he took a bite of the cornbread. Sweetness coated his tongue. Her mama must have taught her that the way to a man's heart was through his stomach.

"This is great." He chewed and swallowed the tasty treat.

"Thank you." She twisted the ring again then exclaimed in dismay. "Oh, I forgot your coffee."

She was up in a flash. Julianne grabbed the coffee and cup all in one action. Caleb watched her pour the hot liquid before returning the pot to the back of the stove.

As soon as she was seated again he asked her. "Do you know what that ring stands for, Julianne?"

She looked at the ring in question. "It means I'm your wife."

He set his spoon on the table and reached across to capture her hand. Caleb turned the ring watching the gold reflect the sunlight that streamed through the kitchen window. "Yes, it does. What else does it mean to you?"

She tugged on her hand but Caleb refused to release her. "It means I'm yours. I clean the house, cook the meals, and watch after Jonathan."

"Anything else?" He raised his head and searched her face.

"It means I am to do anything you ask me to." She whispered and lowered her lashes.

Caleb rubbed the back of her hand with his thumb, enjoying the softness of her skin. "Come with me." He pulled her to her feet.

"But the food will get cold." She tried again to pull her hand out of his but he hung on tight.

"We won't be gone that long, Julianne. I just want to show you something." Caleb pulled her up and around the table. He led her to the door and outside. On the porch he stopped and pulled her in front of him. He dropped her hand and put both hands on her shoulders.

"See the land?"

She nodded.

"It's yours."

"See the garden?"

Again he waited for her nod.

"It's yours. Everything I have is yours."

He dropped his hands from her shoulders and grabbed her hand again. Caleb led her back into the house. He took her into the bedroom. Julianne stiffened by his side. "See the bed?"

Caleb waited several long moments while she worked up the courage to nod. When she did he announced, "It is yours until you are ready to share it."

He pulled her to the foot of the bed where Jonathan lay sleeping. "See the baby?"

Julianne kept her gaze on the baby and nodded.

"He is ours."

Caleb led her back to the kitchen table. "Julianne, this cabin, the land, even the children are ours. Not just mine, not just yours, but ours. Together. We are married, and to me that means everything I have is yours. You are not my slave and I'm not your master. We are partners, and someday I hope that we will become best friends."

He watched a tear trickle down her face. Gently he led her back to her chair at the table. He knelt beside her and picked up the hand with her wedding band on it.

"My grandmother gave me that ring when I was a little boy. She told me to wear it on a chain around my neck so that it would always be close to my heart until the day I found the lady who would hold my heart and the ring."

A tear fell and ran through both their hands. "That ring means more to me than you will ever know. It means you are my wife, my friend and the woman who holds my heart."

Her head snapped up. "You don't love me."

"You're right. But I plan to. Love is more than a feeling. It's actions, too. Try to forget about the past, Julianne, and try to trust me a little. Can you do that?"

Chapter 6

The next morning Julianne pulled her robe on, deciding to make a more concerted effort to be the kind of wife she thought Caleb wanted. It wasn't as though she'd been asleep. Jonathan had kept her up most of the night. She'd tried to keep him quiet and had succeeded for the most part by draping him over her arm. It seemed to be the only way he found relief from the stomach gripes.

She'd searched her memory all through the night trying to remember if her twin nieces had experienced colic. She didn't think they had but then they had been breast fed, not bottle fed. She would ask Maggie about it when she saw her next.

She began to prepare breakfast long before she heard rapid movements overhead. Caleb descended the stairs in a rush. "You didn't have to make breakfast for me. I could have grabbed something at the cookshack."

"I know. I wanted to." She set a bowl of gravy and a pan of hot biscuits on the table.

Caleb pulled a chair out and sat down. "Merciful goodness. This is manna. Thank you."

His smile warmed her insides.

"I was thinking about going to the river and doing some laundry today." Julianne handed Caleb a plate. She dipped a ladle into the gravy for him. "If you'll collect your dirty clothes, I'll wash yours, too." She sat down across from him.

"I'd rather you wait until I get home this evening. I'll go down with you." He ladled gravy over the three biscuits he'd just split apart.

Julianne tore off a piece of bread. "Why?" She watched him chew his food slowly before answering. Would he be angry with her for questioning his decision? She felt heat fill her face as he studied her.

"There are wild animals in the forest. To get to the river, you have to go through part of the woods. I'm worried you might stumble upon a bear with cubs or a snake, or maybe even a cougar. I'm asking you to wait for your own protection." Caleb didn't continue eating until she nodded.

She didn't want to stumble upon those things either, but she had promised Maggie the laundry would be ready after lunch. Julianne chewed on her bottom lip. Maybe if she carried a big walking stick and made lots of noise nothing would bother her.

"Are you afraid to stay alone, now?"

Julianne raised her gaze to his. "No. If I stay close to the house, do you think I'll be okay?"

He gathered up his coat and hat. "You'll be fine. Just

don't pick up any cute or cuddly animals." Caleb opened the door to leave.

"I won't." She followed him out onto the porch.

Caleb turned to her. "Are you sure you'll be okay? You can always come with me, and I'll drop you off at the cookshack."

Julianne dusted imaginary flour from her apron. "No, I'll be fine here." She couldn't bring herself to meet his gaze.

He pulled her into his arms and gave her a quick hug. "I'll see you tonight, then." Caleb released her and headed for the barn and his horse.

Was that a flicker of pride she'd seen in his eyes?

Julianne didn't think he'd be too proud of her if he knew her plans for the morning.

As soon as he rode away and she was certain he wasn't coming back, Julianne rushed back inside to her bedroom. She pulled the bag of dirty clothes from under her bed.

The odor from the soiled clothes stung her nose, and she made a mental note to hide them someplace else. What if Caleb got a whiff of them?

"Jonathan, you and I have a lot of work to do today." She peered into the crib, talking in a soothing voice, hoping he would wake in a good mood. "I'm glad you can't talk. You'd tell on me for sure." She changed his diaper with experienced speed.

The baby hadn't played a part in her earlier plans, and now she had to figure out how to do the laundry and watch him at the same time. She carried Jonathan to the kitchen and warmed milk for his bottle.

"You'll just have to come with me." She squirted a couple of drops of milk on the inside of her wrist to test that it wasn't too hot. Satisfied, she popped the bottle into the baby's mouth. Her mind worked as he drank. "I can pull the bag behind me and carry you. But how am I going to get the clean clothes back without dragging them and getting them dirty again?" Julianne gently chewed the inside of her lip.

Jonathan emptied the bottle and his eyes began to drift shut.

"Oh, no you don't, little man. You have to be burped first." She draped a dish towel over her shoulder and then laid the baby against it. As she patted his back, her gaze moved about the room. A large basket sat in one corner full of blankets and extra bedding.

Jonathan burped and the sound scared him. He flailed his little arms and in the process, grabbed a strand of her hair. Julianne chuckled, and patiently untangled his fingers as she placed him on her bed.

She picked up the basket and dumped its contents beside him. "This will work nicely." She scooped him up, blankets and all, and laid him in the basket. Satisfied he would be okay, Julianne picked up the basket and baby, testing the weight.

They were a little heavy but she felt sure she could make it to the river and back with no problems. Julianne balanced the basket on her hip and bent down to grab the bag of laundry.

"This isn't so bad. I can do this." Julianne made it to the door. She dropped the laundry bag and opened the heavy wooden door, pulled the bag through, dropped it again and closed the door. Beads of sweat trickled down her spine. Julianne glanced down at the baby. He slept soundly with a small thumb securely in his mouth.

She blew pent-up air from her lungs, picked up the bag again and pulled it down the steps and across the yard.

The thought of cougars, bears and snakes slowed her footsteps. Would Caleb lie to keep her from leaving the house? Was it a deliberate manipulation of her thoughts, much as her uncle used to make her do as he wanted? She remembered the serious expression on his face as he'd offered his explanation this morning.

Caleb was a man of God. Julianne knew deep in her heart he hadn't lied to her. She forced her fears back and began to quote the twenty-third psalm.

"'The Lord is my shepherd; I shall not want. He maketh me to lie down in green pastures; he leadeth me beside the still waters. He restoreth my soul; he leadeth me in paths of righteousness for his name's sake. Yea, though I walk through the valley of the shadow of death, I will fear no evil; for thou art with me; thy rod and thy staff comfort me. Thou preparest a table before me in the presence of mine enemies; thou anointest my head with oil; my cup runneth over. Surely goodness and mercy shall follow me all the days of my life; and I will dwell in the house of the Lord forever.'"

Julianne swallowed hard. She thought about the words she'd just spoken. They were the only verses she knew, and at the moment they didn't give her a sense of well-being. Still, she mentally repeated the words as she stepped into the darkness of the woods.

Unease washed over her. Julianne knew she'd misled Caleb with her nod when he'd told her not go into the woods without him. But she comforted herself that she really didn't say she wouldn't go. She'd nodded and that could have meant she understood what he was saying.

She left the path and entered the tall trees. The shade

from their branches immediately cooled her brow and made her feel better. Movement in the underbrush quickened her footsteps.

Julianne forced herself not to run. She focused on the sunshine that peeked through the trees in front of her. The weight of the laundry bag pulled on her arm and snagged on every root on the forest floor.

The sound of running water met her ears. As soon as she exited the trees, Julianne saw the source of the sound.

The river rushed along in front of her. A small shallow stream broke off from the main body, making it the perfect place to do laundry.

She set the baby down by the water's edge, but not too close. Rolling her skirt up at the waist, she waded out to a big protruding rock, and then bent and tied the drawstring bag to her leg. Warm water sloshed about her body. She hadn't realized until she'd entered the water that it must be some branch of a hot spring.

The wet clothes became a heavy pull against her body, but most of the stench would be gone by the time she applied the soap and scrubbed them against a rock. She'd hang the clean clothing on the bushes that lined the riverbank.

Lost in the mundane task, Julianne recalled Caleb's warning of the dangers if she strayed too far from the cabin. What would he do if he found out she'd disobeyed him? The thought of the woodshed behind the cabin came to mind, and she shivered in spite of the heat.

Her face burned as she remembered his quick hug this morning. He'd made her feel like a woman. A desirable woman. Would she be treated like a child for disobeying him?

She allowed her subconscious thoughts to surface.

Since the death of her parents, fear and abuse had been her constant companions. Her uncle had not only beaten her, he'd also told her she was no better than a servant. The mental abuse had been worse than the physical. The most hurtful thing of all had been her aunt's willing consent to this treatment, always quoting Bible passages about discipline. Was this the way Caleb believed? If so, she was in a heap of trouble and the woodshed could be the least of it. Julianne scrubbed the clothes, unaware of the passage of time.

Jonathan's whimpering pulled her from her reflections. She straightened. Arching her back, she looked up into the afternoon sky. Had she really been washing clothes that long? Drying clothes rested over rocks and branches all around her. Her back and neck ached from leaning over the water.

Since Jonathan didn't appear in too much distress, she decided to finish the last two shirts. She knew he had to be hungry and wet. She'd forgotten clean diapers, and not realizing the laundry would take so long, she'd counted on the bottle she'd fed him earlier to be sufficient until she returned to the cabin.

The whimpering turned into angry screeches, and she hurried from the water with the two now-clean shirts. As she passed the basket, she looked at the baby, torn between caring for him and finishing her job. His little face had turned bright red and he waved his fist about.

"I'm sorry, Jonathan," she called, hoping her voice would calm him. She hung the garments and began to gather the dry ones, folding them and laying them on a fairly clean rock on the river bank.

She raised her voice to cover the wails now interspersed with gasps for breath, he was crying so hard.

"I'm hurrying, sweetheart. We'll be home in a few minutes."

She turned her back on him and continued to fold the clothes. A sense of inadequacy swept over her. Maybe this job was too much for her.

But you've done this since you were twelve, her mind argued. Everything was so new to her. Baby Jonathan, Caleb. This vast Washington territory. She should take it easy and get used to things before taking on such a venture. Her husband had paid her debt. She was free. If she didn't want to, she didn't have to do laundry.

But you owe him, her conscience nagged.

Jonathan's cries stopped. She heard him sucking and sighed. "Poor baby." He had a habit of sucking his fist when the bottle didn't get there fast enough. Julianne knew it would be a short reprieve, so she hurriedly folded the last shirt and turned toward the baby.

"No!" The guttural cry tore from her throat.

Chapter 7

The Indian woman looked up from the baby at her breast. White teeth flashed as a smile trembled through the tears running down her face. Two braves stood guard behind her, their arms crossed over their chests. Julianne stumbled toward them, sheer black fright building fearful images in her mind. She fell on her knees in front of the woman.

She pointed at Jonathan whose small fist clasped the woman's hand, which lay protectively on the side of his head. The sound of slurping blended in with the gentle lapping of water.

"Mine," Julianne stammered. "He's mine." Blood rushed to her head causing the breath to squeeze from her lungs. She placed a finger against the pulse in her neck to stem the rapid flow. She would *not* pass out now.

Julianne reached for Jonathan, and one of the men

stepped forward in silent threat. She sat back on her heels waiting for a blow that didn't come. She looked up into the face of the warrior closest to her and wondered what tragedy could bring such sorrow to a person's eyes. Neither man made another move; they just stood silently, watching the young woman feed Jonathan.

Fresh tears joined the tracks already on the woman's face. She nodded once and brushed the hair off Jonathan's forehead. Long after Jonathan fell asleep, she gently removed the baby from her breast and held him out for Julianne to take.

Afraid she might change her mind Julianne snatched him to her chest, rocking back and forth, barely stopping the moan threatening to escape. Her gaze moved back to the men. Displeasure showed briefly in their expressions before they melted into the trees, taking the woman with them.

Julianne began to shake and found it difficult to stand. Keeping her eyes on the forest where the Indians disappeared, she backed toward the river. As quickly as her trembling body would allow, she tossed the clothes and empty bag into the basket. She laid Jonathan on top of the clean clothes and ran back through the woods to the cabin. Her heart pounded and her chest felt as if it might burst as she hurried up the steps and through the door.

Inside, Julianne set the basket and baby on the floor and dropped the bar over the door. Would it be enough to keep the Indians out?

She scooped up Jonathan and hugged him close. He was so tiny and she'd put him in grave danger. When had the baby become a part of her? Never in her life had she been so afraid for another human being.

He cried out at being awakened so roughly. Julianne didn't mind the noise. She was just thankful he was safe as she changed his diaper. Even after his eyes began to close, she refused to put him down. Julianne stared into his face, memorizing his precious features. She'd put him in danger by her disobedience. A beating in the woodshed wouldn't begin to erase the pain in her heart if something had happened to her baby.

Her baby. She felt a mother's intense love for this child. The shock of this discovery hit her full force, and she took a quick breath of utter astonishment.

Someone began pounding on the door.

Julianne jumped from the chair, then froze, fearful the slightest movement might alert the person outside to her whereabouts in the cabin. Had the Indians followed her home? Had the woman changed her mind and returned for the baby? Well, they could not have him. She looked around the room for a weapon of some type.

"Julianne, let me in." Maggie's voice penetrated the door and the fear.

Her relief altered instantly into action. She ran across the room, opened the heavy door and pulled Maggie inside.

"What took you so long? I've got to get back and start supper for those men. Wish I had more time to jaw with you, but I don't." She looked into Julianne's face. "What's wrong girl?"

Julianne placed the bar back into the metal slots on each side of the door.

"Nothing. I'm just tired." Julianne hugged Jonathan's small warm body to her. The lie tasted bitter on her tongue, but she didn't want to tell anyone about the scare she'd experienced.

Worry laced Maggie's face. "Has the little tyke been giving you a hard time?"

"A little." Julianne smoothed the shirt over his small back.

"Well, it does my old heart good to see you caring for him as if he were your own. I was afraid you might not take to the little feller. Here, why don't you let me hold him while you get those clothes ready?" Reluctantly Julianne transferred Jonathan's warm body into Maggie's waiting arms. Maggie took the baby and sat in one of the kitchen chairs.

Her eyes followed Julianne's movements. "You look plumb tuckered out."

"I am a little." Julianne carefully placed the clean clothes into the drawstring bag that was still a bit damp. "The baby doesn't sleep well at night. He seems to have a permanent tummy ache that keeps him from resting both day and night. Is there something I can mix with his milk to help him, or should I water it down so it isn't so strong?"

"Well he seems to be okay right now."

Julianne glanced briefly at Jonathan then jerked her gaze back to him. He lay quietly in Maggie's arms staring up at her, his eyes wide and alert. Julianne rushed to Maggie's side. "Hello there, JoJo," she cooed softly. He turned his head toward her but his eyes never focused. She kept her voice quiet and gentle, barely able to contain the happiness at seeing him so peaceful. "You're feeling better, yes you are." He turned his head to Maggie's chest and closed his eyes. In seconds he was asleep, his tiny legs stretched out, no sign of pain in his tummy.

Julianne went back to finish packing the laundry bag.

"There has to be an easier way to do the laundry." She muttered more to herself than Maggie.

"That bad, eh?"

Jonathan whimpered. Julianne's gaze darted to the baby. Maggie gently jiggled him in her arms.

"When we came up with this idea, I hadn't planned on having a baby to take care of, too." She set the bag down by Maggie's chair.

The older woman stood to leave. She handed Jonathan over with a quick kiss to the forehead. "Well, you'll get used to it. Women been taking care of their children and doing the laundry at the same time for many a moon."

"Maggie, is there an Indian tribe nearby?" Julianne adopted a nonchalant pose, needing to confide the afternoon's scare, but uncertain if Maggie would mention it to Caleb or not. If she could ascertain whether she and Jonathan were safe, then she'd continue the wash as if nothing had happened. On the other hand…

"Why, sure there is. Didn't you see the traders and the Indian men down at the wharf? I'd say they're closer to you than the town, though, seeing as how they travel the canal right at the foot of yer hill." She shuffled to the door, clumsily hefting the bag to her shoulder. "Why'd you ask? Did you see something?"

"No," Julianne noticed that the lie slipped out much easier than the first lie she had told. "I just noticed some marking at the foot of the hill where I wash clothes, and they looked like Indian. I wondered if I should be afraid."

"'Bout the only time I've seen the Injuns in these parts get stirred up was when some no-count white man was a doing the stirring."

Julianne lifted the bar and Maggie swung the wooden door open.

"No reason to fret on their account. There's no danger from the redskin people. It's those good-fer-nothings at the sawmill you gotta worry about." Maggie's features turned to stone as she picked up the bag and left before Julianne could reply.

"Now, what do you suppose got into her craw?" she asked the sleeping baby as she shut the door and dropped the bar into place.

Julianne spent the rest of the afternoon straightening the cabin and cooking dinner. She took a piece of fatback and placed it in the pot of beans boiling on the woodstove. When the meal was nearly ready, she slid a pan of yeast bread into the oven, and soon the smell of fresh-baked bread filled the air.

As she worked, she pondered Caleb's words from the day before. He'd said the house was hers and he'd given her Jonathan. She examined her feelings and realized for the first time in her life, she felt a bottomless peace and satisfaction. The scare this afternoon had shown her that she had a lot to be thankful for. She had a home and a husband—sort of—and she had a son. A sense of strength came to her, and Julianne determined to turn over a new leaf. To do things right. Was this what people meant when they said they had gotten saved? Or made a decision? She decided right then to be a better person. One that Caleb could depend on and be proud of.

She wiped her hands on her apron and went to the window for what seemed like the hundredth time. The sun had already set, and gray streaks of night mingled with the last light of day. Worry began to gnaw at her newfound confidence.

Where was Caleb?

He'd said he would try to get home early and take her

to the river to do laundry. Not that she still needed to do it, but he didn't know that.

Julianne paused and stood perfectly still, listening intently for the sound that had pegged her attention. There it was again. A tinkling like that of a bell. She leaned into the window and squinted to see more clearly. The sound grew closer until she could make out two dark forms coming toward the house.

Had the Indians returned? She scooped up Jonathan and held him close.

"Julianne!" Caleb's rich voice called to her.

Julianne hurried out the door. She made out Caleb on his horse, and he was leading a cow toward the house. The moon crept from behind the clouds long enough for her to see a bell around the cow's neck.

"What do you think of her?" Caleb asked when he came even with the porch. He slid off his horse.

Julianne cuddled the baby closer still. "I think it's a cow."

"Not just any cow. This here is Maybell, and she's our new milk cow." Caleb patted the beast on the neck.

"Maybell? You named her?" Julianne tilted her head to search Caleb's face.

His resonant laughter filled the night. Caleb led the horse and cow toward the barn. "No, I didn't name her. The little son of the farmer I bought her from named her. The man assures me we can get at least three gallons of milk a day from her. What do you think of that?" He pushed the barn door open and led the animals inside.

Julianne followed him into the barn.

He closed the animals into separate stalls, unsaddled his horse and fed and watered them both.

"Caleb?"

He closed the stall door and turned to face her. "What's wrong, honey?"

The concern in his voice and the way he called her *honey* drew Julianne's affection-deprived body to him. She fought an overwhelming need to be in his arms. Surely this all stemmed from the scare she'd had earlier. You couldn't grow close to someone in less than a week. She heaved a sigh. She hated to disappoint him again, but she didn't see how not to, so she blurted it out.

"I don't know how to milk a cow." She tried to stop the trembling of her lower lip.

Caleb put an arm around her shoulders and turned her toward the door. "Well, I do, and I'll teach you."

"Thank you." Her appreciation sounded stiff and unnatural even to her own ears.

Caleb felt her pull away from him. He gently dropped his arm from her shoulders.

"Dinner is ready." Her voice came out as a sigh of relief.

It troubled him that she felt ill at ease in his presence. "I'll get washed up." He headed for the side of the house where the well stood.

Pouring cold water into a basin, Caleb prayed. *Lord, I can't make this woman trust me, and I can't make her like me either. I know I'm supposed to love her, but she's making it awful hard when she shimmies away from me like a horse in a bed of rattlers. Please help us both to grow in your love. Amen.* He finished his quick sponge bath and hurried into the house.

As he entered the front door, Caleb remembered he'd promised to take her to the river to wash clothes. "I'm sorry, Julianne. I plumb forgot about taking you to the river."

She held Jonathan in one arm and served dinner with the other. "That's okay, Caleb. I'm sure you have your reasons for being late."

Her tight voice and the way she clung to the baby expressed in more than words to Caleb that his new wife was unhappy with him. "We can go tomorrow, if you would like to. The boss gave me a couple of days off." Caleb didn't tell Julianne the foreman had given him the time off because he thought they needed a honeymoon.

Julianne waited for him to bless the meal before answering. "That will be fine."

They ate in silence. Julianne continued to hold the baby long after he'd finished his bottle and gone to sleep. Caleb wasn't sure what had gotten into her. The day before, she'd only picked up little Jonathan when he'd needed a clean diaper or if she was feeding him. What had caused the change?

As soon as the last spoonful of beans reached his mouth she started clearing the table. Caleb thought about whittling but changed his mind. He watched her move the baby from one arm to the other as she worked.

He stood and walked over to the basin of water where she washed dishes. "Here let me have the baby for a while. I haven't seen him all day."

Caleb found himself looking deeply into the blue eyes turned up at him. It seemed she was reluctant to hand the baby over to him. For a brief moment, he thought he saw fear, but then relief seemed to wash over her expression.

The baby snuggled into his chest and sighed heavily. Caleb carried him to the table and took a good look at the chairs. What Julianne and the baby needed was a good rocker. Caleb decided he'd make them one, with butterflies and puppies in a field of flowers carved into the high back.

"How are the baby's bottles holding out?" He sat down at the table and studied his nephew's little face.

Julianne wiped her hands on a cloth. "The bottles are okay, it's the nipples I'm worried about. I washed them this afternoon but they still look and smell pretty bad."

Caleb looked up. "I'll start making him a new one tomorrow. Do you think the others will last until I can get it made?"

"Depends on how long it takes. What are you going to make it out of?" Julianne rubbed at the small of her back.

"I'll whittle it out of wood. Shouldn't take but a day, maybe two." His thoughts turned to the rocker. It would have to wait until the new nipple was finished. He glanced up to find Julianne staring at him.

Concern laced her tired blue eyes and tiny lines marred her forehead. "Oh, Caleb, the splinters will hurt his little mouth and besides he won't be able to suck a wooden nipple."

Caleb stood up and took the baby to his crib. "I'll make sure it's smooth and the hole will be very tiny so that he won't get too much milk at one time." He turned back to the kitchen and bumped into Julianne who had followed him closely to the cradle.

She tried to back out of his grasp, but her feet tangled up with his boots and he felt them both falling.

Caleb twisted his body, barely feeling the soft bed beneath him as Julianne landed on his chest. Air whooshed from his lungs.

Her dark hair covered his face, and she let out a little

squeak. Caleb felt her hands on his chest and the pressure she applied as she pushed herself up.

For reasons he didn't know or understand, Caleb wrapped his arms around her and held her close. He stared up into startled baby-blue eyes.

Julianne's dark hair created a curtain around their faces. Her sweet breath mixed with his. Their lips paused, mere inches apart.

Chapter 8

Julianne felt the movement of his breathing beneath her. His compelling green eyes stared up at her, questions glittering in their debts.

"Would it be too much for a husband to ask for a kiss, sweet Julianne?" His whole being seemed to be filled with waiting.

She noticed he watched her mouth intently. His hand moved from her waist to pick up a curl and rub it between his finger and thumb. He brought her untried senses to life. Where her voice came from, Julianne wasn't sure. She heard herself whisper. "I am your wife, Caleb. If you want a kiss, all you have to do is take it."

Caleb dropped the captured curl and gently set her from him. "I won't take your kisses. They are something you will freely give or I won't have them." He pushed himself off the bed and left the cabin.

Disappointment worked its way into her confused thoughts. He hadn't kissed her. She let out a long audible sigh. Julianne thought men always took what they wanted. Caleb hadn't. Confusion filled her mind. She hadn't wanted him to take the kiss, and yet she felt the need to sample one from him.

She quickly changed into her nightgown and prepared for bed. After brushing her hair, she climbed under the quilts.

Why hadn't he kissed her? She flipped over onto her stomach. The thoughts troubled her. Why did she care that he hadn't kissed her?

"I should be grateful." She breathed into the pillow. But, she wasn't. Julianne chalked it up to being overly tired from her day at the stream.

Caleb left the house torn by conflicting emotions. She had made him sound like a caveman. "'I'm your wife; all you have to do is take it.'" He mimicked her words out loud.

Didn't she know he wouldn't force himself on her? Hadn't he told her as much?

Disappointment ate at him. Her breath and hair had smelled fresh and clean. Everything about her seemed pure.

Caleb admitted he'd wanted the kiss. What would it be like to touch her sweet lips with his?

He stomped out to the barn. The horse neighed, and the cow mooed. Caleb picked up the lantern that sat on a small shelf by the door and lit it.

He walked over to his horse and rubbed its nose. "I don't understand my new wife."

The cow released a low sound that snagged Caleb's

sense of humor, and he chuckled in spite of himself. "Oh, you understand her do you?" He moved across the stall and scratched behind the cow's big velvet ear.

"For just a moment, I was sure she wanted the kiss as much as I did." He moved away from the animals to a pile of wood that sat at the back of the barn.

Caleb searched through it until he found a small piece of wood. He carried it back to the old stump he used as a stool. A knife lay on the ledge close by and he picked it up and began to whittle.

Prayers peeled from his soul with each shaving of wood.

How long he whittled and prayed Caleb wasn't sure. He held the small nipple out and looked it over. A good roll in river sand would soften the edges of the wood and make it safe for the baby.

He stood, blew out the lantern and returned to the cabin.

Careful not to wake Julianne, he climbed the stairs to his bed. The mattress creaked with his weight. Caleb wondered if Julianne had heard. He tilted his head sideways and listened.

The cabin remained silent. Tomorrow would be different, he told himself. It was obvious Julianne didn't trust him. He had to nurture her until she did. With that thought in mind, he drifted off to sleep.

Heat bore down on him until he thought he would suffocate. Caleb twisted in the quilt. Sleep evaporated from his eyes, and he sat up. Daylight filtered through the window, and he realized he'd overslept.

He ran a hand through his damp hair. The house was stifling hot, and he wondered what had caused such heat. Pulling his clothes on, Caleb started down the stairs.

When he got to the bottom he found the house empty. Fresh loaves of bread rested on the kitchen table, but Julianne and the baby were nowhere to be found, so he went in search of them.

Stepping onto the porch he realized it was almost noon. He'd slept away most of the day. What must Julianne think of him? Where was she, anyway?

He scoured the yard and garden. He didn't see her anywhere, and his heart began to pound.

The cow let out a loud bellow. Caleb ran to the barn. He stopped just outside the open doors. Who was inside the barn? Could the Indians have come to carry off his family, livestock, and who knew what else, while he slept?

It took all his will not to race inside when he heard Julianne's raised voice. He could sense the anger in her.

"Fine! See if I try to help you again. You are an ungrateful beast with a nasty temper."

Caleb cautiously peeked around the door. His lovely wife stood with her hands on her hips, facing the cow, who had her head lowered and looked ready to charge.

"Don't even think about it. We'll be having steaks for dinner if you dare," she threatened the animal.

Pride filled Caleb's chest at his wife's bravery. He could see the cow's eyes were just as determined as Julianne sounded. The animal lifted her head and shook the bell around her neck.

"Good morning." Caleb came further into the barn.

Julianne turned. Dirt splattered her dress and hay poked out of different places in her hair. Smudges of gook and something dark lined one cheek. Her blue eyes flashed in anger.

"Lord, you sure are a beauty when you're mad."

The words popped out of his mouth before he could stop them.

If it were at all possible, her eyes glinted even brighter. Her face flushed a bright red, and her nostrils flared. Caleb wasn't sure if the flush was from embarrassment or anger, but it made her even more appealing to him.

"I am not mad. I'm angry. Dogs go mad and foam at the mouth. Do you see me foaming at the mouth?" she demanded.

She had tied a sheet across one shoulder and baby Jonathan rested inside its folds. Caleb watched her cuddle the baby closer to her as she waited for his answer.

"No ma'am. I don't see any foam." He wanted to laugh but didn't dare. She looked so beautiful with hay in her hair and her eyes that incredible shade of ice blue.

"Good." A smile tilted the corners of her mouth.

Caleb couldn't contain the laughter. It bubbled from his throat and washed away some of the rejection of the night before.

Her laughter joined his. "I was trying to get that ornery animal to let me milk her. Her udder is full but she won't allow me to touch her."

He picked up the milk pail and the stump he'd sat on the night before. "Maybell, why won't you let the pretty lady milk you?" Caleb walked to the cow and pulled her out into the yard.

His eyes swept over Julianne approvingly as he passed her. She was so unaware of the captivating picture she made with her hair all mussed up and the red spots dotting her cheeks. He bit his lip to stifle a grin.

Julianne followed. He heard her soft footsteps behind him.

"How is it you've never milked a cow before?" He

sat the stump on the ground and pulled the cow forward until her udder was in line with the stump.

"The opportunity never presented itself. We lived in the city and our milk was delivered each morning."

"I remember delivered milk in the morning." He walked quickly into the barn, a satisfied smile pulling at the corner of his mouth when he turned and she was right on his heels.

"You do?"

He nodded.

"Do you ever miss New York?" Her question caused him a moment of concern. Was she perhaps longing for home? He answered carefully.

"There are certain things I miss." He lifted a handful of hay from the haystack at the back of the barn. "Like milk delivered to the door in the morning; reading *Harper's* magazine on Sunday mornings." He strode back to Maybell and dropped the hay in front of her. "I miss the theater."

Julianne clapped her hands. "Oh, me too. Did you ever visit the Crystal Palace?" Her voice rose an octave in excitement.

"No, I never made it there. Whenever I found time to escape I went to the Astor."

"Yes, yes, I loved the Astor Library. I didn't get to go often but when the opportunity arose, I went and stayed for hours at a time." Caleb noticed her mood seemed suddenly buoyant, a distinct change from when they'd entered the barn.

"Do you miss it very much?" Caleb purposefully kept his voice without inflection but he couldn't stop himself from studying her face.

She looked away hastily, then moved restlessly. She

sighed and gave a resigned shrug. "I miss the things we mentioned. I even miss my family. But not enough to ever want to go back." When she lifted her eyes pain flickered briefly in their beautiful depths.

Caleb knew about pain. He and his sister had been alone most of their lives, scrambling to just get by. When Estelle married it was a great match and he was finally free to live whatever lifestyle he chose. The West had called to him and he'd set out to make a new beginning for himself.

"We lived down near the wharf in lower Manhattan. There was never a quiet moment with the ships arriving all times of the day and night. There were lots of guttersnipes and no law most of the time. I managed to keep my sister in school and involved in the best culture I could supply. When she married I hightailed it out of there as fast as I could. I knew I could make a good life for myself if I ever got the chance."

"So you never want to go back?" Julianne's voice sounded strained, but she seemed to be preoccupied with Maybell's placement over the bucket he'd set under her. With sudden clarity he knew his answer was very important to her. He chose his words carefully.

"I won't say I will *never* go back again, but I have no plans to in the next ten years or so. Maybe one day, if Jonathan wants to go to West Point, I might visit my hometown again." He watched the stiffness leave her shoulders and after a long pause he stated firmly. "My home is here now, and I love every inch of our place. I feel blessed of the Lord to have accomplished several of the things I longed to do when I came West."

She answered him in a rush of words. "You've done a wonderful job, Caleb. You're still young, yet you have more material possessions than any of the other saw-mill workers. And the house is lovely. Even this barn proves that your dedication to hard work and persever-ance has paid off."

"Are you proud of your husband, Julianne?" He teased her, feeling the need to lighten the mood.

Standing on tiptoe, she touched her lips to his. Her feather-light touch seared a path to his soul. "There isn't a woman alive more proud of her husband." Stains of scar-let appeared on her cheeks and she dropped her hands quickly from his shoulders.

"Why don't I get Maybell something more to eat, and then I'll show you how it's done."

This time Julianne nodded. She pressed the baby closer to her and waited while Caleb entered the barn and returned with more hay for the cow to chew on. While they'd been preoccupied with each other, May-bell had gone to town on her food.

After giving the cow more hay, Caleb repositioned the bucket under her udder and sat down on the stump. He showed Julianne how to milk the cow. "See? That's not so hard is it?" He glanced up in time to catch her gnawing on her lower lip.

She shrugged uncertainly. Caleb stood to his feet. "Here, sit down, and I'll teach you."

Julianne did as instructed.

Caleb watched her tuck the baby close to her body and lean forward. She took a teat in her hand and squeezed.

Maybell let out a loud moo. Caleb saw fire and a chal-lenge rush into Julianne's eyes.

"Don't start," she ordered the cow, then she looked up at him with those bright eyes. "I don't think she likes my touch as much as she does yours."

He chuckled. "She's used to me milking her. She'll get used to you, too. Just give her time."

"But, I thought you bought her yesterday, how come she's used to you already?"

"I picked her up yesterday. I bought her a couple of weeks ago, and the previous owners agreed to house her till the hay I ordered arrived. I wanted my own fresh milk and butter, so I've been going to their place to do the milking."

"Oh, that explains the fresh milk."

"Yes, and it shows how the Lord provides before we even have a need." At her questioning look, he clarified. "I would never have dreamed my sister would pass away leaving me with a baby that had to be fed. But He knew, and now Jonathan is taken care of. God provides for his children."

Julianne seemed to concentrate for a moment on what he had said, then leaned forward and tried again.

Maybell stomped the ground with her hind leg.

Caleb moved behind Julianne and placed a hand over hers. "Here let me help you."

His hand engulfed hers. Caleb marveled at the difference in their sizes.

The smell of lavender from her hair floated up to him with the heat from the sun. He moved their hands together and showed her how to pull so that the milk would come out. He was unaware of the lesson, only of the woman in front of him.

After several moments of pulling, Caleb felt her body ease back against him. He gently scooted her forward on the stump and sat down behind her.

Jonathan woke from his morning nap. His sleepy gaze met Caleb's.

"He's growing fast." Caleb drew her closer to him by putting his left arm around her waist.

Julianne worked with both hands now. Caleb released her right hand and completely circled her in his arms.

"This is fun."

Caleb wondered if she meant the milking or being in his arms. He bent his head and nuzzled his face into the hair at her neck. She angled her head to accommodate his touch and the slender, delicate thread that had formed between them strengthened. She drew him like a magnet.

"Well now, iffen this ain't right cozy."

Julianne shot up from their seat on the stump. "Maggie, I wasn't expecting you to visit today."

Caleb caught the bucket before it spilled. He stood slowly, bringing the milk with him. "Morning, Maggie. Come on, Maybell. I'll take you out back where there's fresh grass."

"I can see you weren't." He heard Maggie's laughter as he headed behind the barn.

Julianne stared after Caleb. His broad shoulders and narrow waist set her heart to pounding. The strength in his arms was matched by the even stronger strength of his character. For a few brief moments, she had felt safe in his arms.

Maggie's voice pulled Julianne from her thoughts. "He's quite a man isn't he? I'd have chased him myself, if I was a few years younger."

Heat filled Julianne's face. Were her thoughts that obvious? She turned away from the inquisitive look on Maggie's face.

Jonathan wiggled around in the blanket. He gave a

small cry, and Julianne felt moisture against her stomach. She sighed. He needed changing again.

"Would you like to come inside while I change the baby?" Julianne asked.

At Maggie's nod they headed for the house. Julianne pulled the door open and slipped behind the curtain that divided the bedroom from the main room.

Maggie ladled two glasses full from the water bucket in the kitchen. "I came out to ask if you and Caleb will be attending services tomorrow."

Caleb had not mentioned it to Julianne. She changed the baby, then pulled the damp dress over her head and slipped into her last clean one. She pulled another half-sheet from the pile of clean clothes and tied it over her shoulder. She settled Jonathan comfortably against her chest and patted his bottom.

As she entered the kitchen, Maggie handed her a glass of water. Julianne said, "I don't know if we'll go to services tomorrow. Does Caleb usually attend church on Sunday?"

"He usually does, but I wasn't sure if he would this Sunday."

"Why wouldn't he?" Julianne set the glass on the table and rearranged Jonathan in the sheet. She patted his back as she waited for Maggie to answer.

The older woman shrugged her shoulders. "Well, with you two just being married and all…I thought maybe…" She looked pointedly at the curtained-off bedroom area.

Heat filled Julianne's face once more. She moved to the cabinet and started putting clean dishes away. "I'm sure we will be going." Julianne couldn't bring herself to face Maggie.

What would her friend say if she knew they weren't really man and wife? Julianne chewed her bottom lip.

"Where will we be going?" Caleb asked.

Julianne's gaze shot to the door. How long had he been standing there? Had he heard Maggie's comment?

"I was just asking Julianne if you two are going to services in the morning." Maggie sat down.

Caleb's gaze continued to hold Julianne's. "We'll be there."

Maggie smiled at them. "Tomorrow is the annual picnic. I love the annual picnic. It's one of the few days of the year I don't have to eat my own slop."

Julianne pulled her gaze away from Caleb. "What should I take?" She snuggled Jonathan close to her chest.

"Lots of food. There will be plenty of loggers and only a few ladies there. Which reminds me, I need to get back to camp and start on my food for tomorrow." Maggie stood to her feet.

Caleb stepped to the side of the door to allow her room to pass.

"I'll see you two tomorrow." Maggie waved as she left.

Julianne followed her to the porch. "Thanks for coming by, Maggie. Please, come again soon."

Maggie climbed up onto her horse and surprised Julianne by straddling his back. The older woman gathered the reins in her hands and winked at Julianne. "Thanks, I will." She turned the horse and galloped out of sight.

Julianne's thoughts raced. She had to wash clothes so that she would have a clean dress for tomorrow. There was food that needed to be prepared and she needed a bath.

Jonathan began to fuss.

"And you need to be fed." She pulled the baby closer to her and bounced him.

Caleb came to stand beside her. "I'll feed him for you, Julianne."

"Thanks but I can do it." She returned to the kitchen and prepared the baby's bottle. The rubber nipple smelled bad and no longer fit the bottle correctly.

"Maybe this will fit better." Caleb held out a little wooden nipple.

Julianne jumped at the sound of his voice. He stood so close she could smell the earthy scent of him. Her gaze moved to the small nipple and the large, hand that held it out.

"Thank you." She took the nipple and fitted it onto the bottle. Julianne examined the tiny hole in the top of it. She turned the full bottle upside down. Small drops of milk landed on her wrist. Not enough to drown the baby but just enough to supply him with the nourishment he needed.

Caleb touched the top of the crying baby's head. "What do you think? Will it work?"

Julianne gave Jonathan the bottle. He began feeding greedily. A small trickle of milk formed at the corner of his little lips.

"Oh, Caleb, this is so much better than the old nipple." Her eyes met his, and she smiled.

A soft grin touched Caleb's firm lips. Julianne focused on his mouth. They were only inches apart, and she leaned toward him.

Their lips met. He felt solid and wonderful. Her heart flipped, and she felt a small piece of it warm towards her new husband.

Julianne pulled away and ducked her head. She carried Jonathan to the table and sat down.

"Thank you for the nipple."

Caleb watched color flood her neck and face. Her voice sounded breathless and appealing. She must have felt the thrill racing through her veins just as he had when their lips touched.

His gaze moved over his small family. Jonathan and Julianne looked like mother and son. She caressed his little head as he drank deeply from the bottle.

A few minutes later, Jonathan protested, needing to burp. He tossed his head back and gave out a loud cry.

Julianne set the half-empty bottle on the table and spoke softly to the baby. "You need to burp, Jonathan. As soon as you do, you'll get to finish your dinner."

"He's a brawny little fellow, isn't he?" Caleb rested one booted foot upon the chair beside her and the baby.

A loud belch filled the room. Jonathan flung his arms out and gave a big wail.

Julianne settled him back into the crook of her arm and returned the bottle to his mouth. "Yes, he is."

Caleb studied them for a few more moments. "When you finish up here, do you want to go down to the stream and wash the clothes?"

"That would be nice. The house is still too hot to start cooking." She rocked from side to side as she fed the baby.

Her gaze met his. Once more, Caleb saw fear in her eyes and wondered what scared her. Was it him? Was he standing too close? Caleb dropped his foot from the chair and stepped back.

Julianne burped the baby again. "I'll be ready in just

a moment," she offered, tucking Jonathan into the folds of the sheet.

Caleb headed toward the door. "Good, I'll check on the horse and cow before we take off." He made his way out the door and headed to the barn.

He worried that she still feared him. What could he do to make her feel safe? Caleb pondered the question as he thrust the pitchfork into the hay and tossed it to the livestock.

A scream filled the hot air. He jerked his head up at the sound.

Julianne.

Panic clawed at his throat, and he whirled to run to the house. Still holding the pitchfork, Caleb raced out of the barn. His heart seemed to leap from his chest in sheer terror. Never had he heard such raw fear rip from a woman's throat.

Chapter 9

Julianne clutched the baby to her. The rattling continued in the corner.

The snake's beady eyes stared at her, and its forked tongue flickered in and out of its mouth. Its body coiled on the floor as the snake raised its head. The rattles sang in the hot, still air.

She pressed the baby tighter to her chest And backed into a kitchen chair. Roaring started in her ears and blackness threatened to overtake her. She fought the weakness of her knees. She couldn't faint. She had to protect Jonathan.

The snake raised its head farther off the floor. It opened its mouth, and two sharp white fangs threatened her.

"Caleb!" She screamed his name. Her throat felt raw from the force of her screams.

The door slammed against the wall with a crash that

shook the cabin. She jumped in alarm. Caleb was there. She saw the pitchfork in his hand.

Julianne's mouth went dry, and her head began to swim. Then a quick and disturbing thought shook her to the core. What if the snake bit Caleb? The thought tore at her insides. Her heart contracted.

The snake's coils slithered around on the floor. Its tail whirred a warning, and its head came up to strike. Only this time, Caleb was its target.

Julianne jerked the tied corners of the sheet that held Jonathan from around her neck. She quickly laid the screaming baby on the kitchen table and turned to see what Caleb and the snake were doing.

The snake's head waved in the air.

"Don't move." Caleb instructed.

Movement had caused the snake to turn on Caleb and movement would distract it from Caleb, too. Julianne prayed she was right. She grabbed the chair behind her and shoved it across the floor toward the snake.

The snake turned and struck at the chair.

Caleb drove the pitchfork through the creature's head.

Julianne gasped.

The snake's body twitched on the kitchen floor. Julianne felt Caleb's gaze skim over her.

"Are you and Jonathan okay?"

Suddenly no sound would come from her throat. She nodded.

Tears tumbled down her face. She ran to Caleb and wrapped her arms around his waist.

"There, there." He enveloped her in his arms and rubbed her back. "You're safe now. I won't let anything hurt you, Julianne."

She sobbed into his chest and held on to him. Safety.

That's what she craved. And with Caleb's strong arms around her, Julianne felt more secure than she'd ever felt in her life.

Her tears were ruining his shirt, but she couldn't stop their flow. She tightened her grip around him. If only she could stay here forever. If only all her fears could be dispensed with as easily as the snake he'd just killed.

Jonathan's protests at being left alone intensified. Julianne sighed. She had to care for the baby, but oh, how she longed to stay right where she was.

She moved to pull from his arms. "The baby needs me," she offered, when he didn't release her.

"The baby is safe." He paused then added, "I need you, too."

She felt him rest his chin on her head. A deep sigh eased from his lungs. Had he held his breath the whole time he faced down the snake? Julianne felt sure he had.

His body trembled around her. Julianne inched her hands up his back and rubbed his shoulders, and for the first time, they took comfort from each other.

Jonathan seemed to realize the danger was over and quieted. He'd cried so hard he had the snubs.

Julianne relaxed in the safety and warmth of Caleb's arms. She replayed the last few minutes through her mind and shuddered. What if Caleb hadn't been home? Or God forbid, if the snake had bitten him, what would she have done without him?

He slowly released her. "I'll get the snake out of here, and then we'll head to the stream. I could use the fresh air."

She watched him move to the snake and pull the pitchfork out of its head. Nausea rose in her throat. Julianne forced herself to really look at the snake now that it no longer moved.

From the tip of its nose to its tail it was almost four feet long Julianne guessed. It was tan with dark brown zigzags marking its length. The head was a diamond shape, and her stomach turned at the memory of the evil in its yellow eyes.

Julianne stored the information away for future use. Caleb carried the snake outside. She hurried to the table. It was her job to protect the baby, and for the second time in two days she'd almost let him come to harm. She silently prayed and asked the Lord to help her be a better mother to her adopted son.

Her gaze moved to the basket that the clothes and snake had been in. She slipped the sheet containing Jonathan back over her head and took a deep breath. Still, her feet refused to move toward the discarded items.

Caleb stood in the doorway. "Let me get that for you."

She watched him flip over the basket and pick up each individual piece of clothing and place it inside.

"I don't think there are any more snakes." He lifted the basket and turned toward her.

Julianne stared at him. Caleb Hanson, her husband, had saved her from the snake. He hadn't been worried about his own safety.

Wonder filled her. He had put her needs above his. No man had ever done that for her. Her insides quivered with the knowledge that he cared for her.

"Ready?"

She saw the concern still expressed in his face. What a ninny she must look like standing here staring at him as if he'd sprouted two horns. Julianne picked up the bag she had prepared earlier for Jonathan and agreed. "Ready."

Caleb led the way down to the stream, his footsteps sure and strong.

With Caleb to protect her, she could enjoy the beauty around her. Little yellow birds sang overhead in the tree branches, and insects fluttered from flower to flower. Julianne took her time and admired the beautiful surroundings.

In her earlier trip, she had raced through, seeing all kinds of dangerous animals and missing the pink flowers and yellow birds. She sighed and inhaled the sweet fragrance of the flowers. Caleb set the basket beside the stream and sorted the clothes. She watched him sink to the bank and begin washing one of her dresses. Julianne hurried and knelt by his side.

"I'll do this." She removed the blue calico from his hands.

She dunked the material into the water expecting Caleb to walk off and occupy his time elsewhere. He didn't move and a splashing sound met her ears just before water droplets landed on her arms. This time he vigorously washed one of his shirts. She sat back on her heels.

"Caleb, you don't have to help me."

He continued to scrub and Julianne frowned. Men didn't scrub clothes. So what was he doing?

Caleb rinsed the soap out of the red shirt and stood to hang it on a nearby bush. Julianne admired his easy movements as he knelt beside her again. Did he think that because she had been afraid of the snake that she couldn't do the wash?

"Really, Caleb," she huffed. "I am capable of doing

the laundry." She bent back to the task of rubbing the soil from the dress.

She heard, more than saw, him sit back. "Julianne." His voice held steel even though he called her name softly.

"What?" Julianne didn't look up.

He pulled on the sheet that held Jonathan to her. "Julianne, look at me."

She did as he said with reluctance. "What, Caleb? I don't have time for games. I have to finish the wash, cook two meals and get a bath today." Julianne dared him to deny what she said.

A warm smile caught her off guard. "I know you have to do those things, and I'm going to help you." He reached up and tucked a wayward curl behind her ear.

"Why? Don't you have something else to do?" She hated the way her voice came out in a whisper. Caleb would think she was weak and unable to take care of the chores.

Laughter filled the air around them. "Nope, I'm here to protect my family and to be a helpmeet to my beautiful wife."

Julianne stared at him. He thought she was beautiful? The man had to be half blind. Her hair fell from the neat bun she'd created this morning, she knew her skin was freckled from being out in the sun without a bonnet, and her dress was wet and muddy at the knees. And besides, wasn't it her job to be the helpmeet to him? He puzzled her, this man she'd married. But he also drew her in ways she couldn't deny. Julianne ducked her head, sure he was teasing her.

The more she was around Caleb the more Julianne knew she was falling in love with this gentle man who was her husband. Her husband.

He startled Julianne by cupping her lowered chin in his strong, callused hand and gently raising her head. Her confused gaze met his warm eyes. She could hardly believe that was truly attraction she saw, and heard in his voice, as he announced, "Julianne, God brought us together to help each other. I'm glad He did."

Julianne was glad, too. Caleb began to talk. As they scrubbed clothes together by the water's edge he told her of his dreams of owning an apple orchard.

"But where would you put an apple orchard? The only cleared space is around the cabin and the garden."

"I'll keep cutting timber as I get time. I want to build more onto the house behind the rooms we have now. That's why I left the roof so high on the back. It will take me several years to clear the acreage but I'm young and strong, and by the time I get the trees removed I'll have the money to buy the seedlings."

"Won't you need help? I mean, I can help out a lot, but I'm not sure I know how to cut down trees." She looked at him anxiously. "I love to plant, though, so I can help when you are ready to do that."

"I'm thinking of asking the boss if he'd like to cut the timber off my property. He can bring the men and they will have several acres cleared in a week. He can keep the money from the sale of the wood."

The excitement in his voice as he described the trees and different kinds of apples he would sell was contagious. Julianne began thinking she and Caleb would make a great team.

How could she help him make his dream come true?

"I want to help so much. It makes me happy to see you so happy."

They had finished the washing and spread the clothes

out on the bushes to dry. Julianne sat down on the log she and the Indian woman had shared. Caleb sat beside her and took her hand. "You know what makes me happier than my plans for an orchard?"

She looked him in the eyes and saw the seriousness of his gaze. Her whole being seemed to be filled with waiting. Her voice came out in a weak and tremulous whisper. "What?"

"Having you to talk to, to share my plans with."

"But that's not helping."

He reached out, turning her to face him. "Let me assure you, you have already helped tremendously." She shook her head and he grasped her chin and his left eyebrow raised a fraction. "I'm not funning at all. Do you know how long it takes me in the evening to fix a meal, to keep the clothes washed and the house cleaned?" He gave an impatient shrug. "You have it all done when I get home. The firewood has been carried in, the water. My meal is ready and the house is clean." His hand pushed a damp curl off her cheek, lingering a moment on her neck.

He leaned back on the log propping himself with his hands behind him. "The loneliness was hardest to bear."

"But you had Maggie and the men from the sawmill. Didn't that help?"

"Sure, when there was work. But it rains so much here and that stops the work. Sometimes a month at a time. Maggie would go into town and stay with friends and I have nothing in common with the men I work with so I'd stay at the house and try and find something to do. That's when I started to whittle."

Julianne knew about loneliness. "Loneliness comes in different forms." At his questioning gaze she continued. "I lived in a house full of people and I felt lonely."

He questioned her about her family and she told him of her parents' death and moving in with her aunt and uncle, the four cousins, all under the age of ten, the twins being born five years later than the older girls. She told him of the work she'd done and the raising of the twins.

"So that's why you looked like you'd eaten unripe persimmons when Maggie handed you Jonathan on the day of the contest." Seeing the amusement in his eyes, she laughed.

"I had no intention of being tied to a baby again."

"And now?" There was an arrested expression on his face as he waited for her answer.

"I could not love him more if I'd given birth to him myself." Julianne spoke with quiet emphasis. "I cannot imagine my life without him."

As their eyes met, she felt a shock run through her. The heartrending tenderness of his gaze wrapped around her like a warm blanket. He felt the same as she did, she could tell, and the idea sent her spirits soaring.

"And me? Could you imagine life without me?"

"I don't want to." Her heart hammered in her ears. Despite his closed expression, she sensed his vulnerability. "The day only starts when you come home to me in the evening."

In one forward motion he wrapped her in his arms. She relaxed, sinking into his embrace. His kiss when it came was slow and thoughtful.

One tiny, furious wail rent the air, pulling them apart. Caleb laughed. "I knew I couldn't keep you to myself much longer." In spite of herself, she chuckled.

Chapter 10

Julianne rocked Jonathan to sleep. Caleb would be home soon. Love for him and the baby swelled in her heart. They had settled into a daily routine without any major glitches to speak of. She marveled at the changes the last two weeks had brought into her life.

Her husband cared for her. He'd shown it in many ways. She loved that Caleb made sure to spend time with her. Every evening they took long walks in the woods and by the river.

Each morning they shared a warm breakfast before he went to work. She would straighten the cabin and then take the laundry down to the river.

Her mind swept back over the events of this morning. As soon as Caleb had left for the sawmill, she'd carried the laundry to the river and before she could set the basket down, the Indian woman and her friend had shown up.

"Hi." Julianne swallowed nervously. She noticed there didn't seem as much tension as at their first meeting.

The woman pointed to Jonathan, then pointed to herself. Julianne thought for a moment before giving her consent. The woman had asked permission this time before holding Jonathan. That showed that she had no evil intent, surely. The brave was there, too, so he could easily demand that Julianne hand over the baby, but instead he waited quietly also. Julianne reached to take Jonathan out of the sling around her neck. She noticed the flicker of relief in the brave's eyes and the soft smile of happiness on the woman's face.

Jonathan began to fret as he was lifted into the other woman's arms. She snuggled his tiny body close and breathed him in, then settled him at her breast. Julianne felt a moment of envy.

"Morning. Star."

Julianne startled. The man gestured toward the woman. "Her name. Morning Star."

"You speak English." Julianne stumbled in her excitement as she stepped toward them.

"Little." He shrugged and a tiny smile tipped up one corner of his mouth. "Name?" When she was slow to comprehend, he pointed at her and repeated, "Name?"

"Oh. Julianne." She kept her words to a minimum, copying him.

"Julie. Anne." He nodded at his wife and repeated Julianne's name to her.

Morning Star dragged her gaze from the baby and looked at Julianne with a smile as bright as the sun. She seemed to look into Julianne's very soul, then she nodded as if coming to some decision and said, "Friend." She lifted Jonathan to her shoulder and patted his little back. His head wobbled back and forth till he settled against her.

The brave wandered slowly upstream leaving the two women alone. Julianne sorted the clothes into two piles, whites and darks. The woman continued to feed Jonathan, paying little attention to Julianne. Julianne wondered what the lady did with her own baby. Did she have so much milk she needed to feed two? And what caused the look of sadness on the faces of both her and her brave? As if she sensed Julianne's questions she burped the baby and laid him in the sling Julianne had placed in the basket after she'd dumped the clothes on the ground.

Julianne tied the clothes bag to her leg and stepped into the water. She looked up in surprise when a splash told her Morning Star had entered the creek with her. To her utter amazement Morning Star picked up a wooden tub that Julianne hadn't noticed before, and dipped it in the stream till it filled. She pointed to Julianne's leg. Julianne bent to untie the bag, fairly certain that's what the Indian woman wanted. She couldn't help the smile pulling at her lips when Morning Star began to shave tiny flecks of soap into the tub of water.

She watched silently as Morning Star took a thick piece of smooth wood and began to joggle the clothes up and down, round and round, till the clothes couldn't be seen for the soap suds. She handed the stick to Julianne and ran up the bank and returned with a second bucket. She filled it full of water then began to wring out the soapy clothes. She shook out each shirt and tossed it in the clean water.

Julianne giggled and grabbed the next load of clothes and washed them while Morning Star rinsed. In barely more than an hour all the clothes were drying on bushes and the buckets were emptied and stashed between two logs back off the bank. Julianne placed her hands on her hips and surveyed all they had accomplished. It had taken her most of the day the last time she'd washed the men's clothing.

"I can't believe we accomplished so much in so little time. And they smell wonderful."

Morning Star raised her eyebrows in question. She sat on the ground, her legs under her, back straight as a rod. Julianne sat down on the other side of the basket where Jonathan slept.

"Work. Fast."

Morning Star smiled and shook her head. "Friends work. Much better."

Julianne leaned back on her hands and lifted her face to the morning sun, which was midway in the sky. Such a beautiful sight to see. Most often it rained or drizzled, but today the bright rays reflected off the water casting an almost blinding light. She felt her spirits rising. She had a friend. Her workload had been much easier today. Surely the Lord was smiling on her.

Julianne had brought two biscuits with pork, and she held one out to Morning Star. Morning Star opened a pouch around her neck and handed a beef jerky strip and a small square of corn bread to Julianne.

"Why you...fear...inside?" Morning Star struggled with her words but her question cut to the quick.

Julianne's hands shook as she sought for simple words her friend would understand. How did you explain to someone from such a different background that your own flesh and blood might do you harm? Before she could form the words Morning Star continued.

"You hur, hurreee," Morning Star stumbled over the

new word, "through woods, looking behind and to side, fearful. Then hurreee to do wash and give small time to play. Why? To hide from your man, yes? I no understand."

Julianne watched a quizzical look cross her friend's face.

"Your man, he is not a man of honor?"

The very question cut to the core of Julianne's heart. She'd thought Morning Star was talking about her uncle; instead, she'd picked up on the very root of Julianne's deception.

"Caleb is an honorable man, Morning Star. The very best." Sorrow ate away at Julianne. She'd cast an unfavorable image of her husband, the man she'd come to love with all her heart. Her own lies had caused this damage.

She jumped to her feet, pacing the river's edge. How could she have done this to a man who had shown her the best things life had to offer? And he'd freely given his trust. What kind of person repaid such kindness like this?

A slight tug on her sleeve drew her attention.

"I not mean to cause friend pain." Morning Star extended her hands toward Julianne. "Please, to have my lunch." She offered her food as an apology.

Julianne smiled and placed an arm around the other woman's shoulder.

"No, you eat your food. You did not upset me." Julianne struggled to maintain an even, conciliatory tone, when she wanted to howl and cry in frustration. "I have been dishonest with my man, and I am ashamed."

"Then you honor him. With trust. A warrior not strong if doubt his woman is loyal."

They began to gather the clothing, silently folding, both seemingly lost in thought. Finally Julianne decided to do a bit of her own questioning. She touched Morning Star's arm to get her attention. She struggled with how to ask the question. Finally she decided a little sign language might help her.

She pointed to Morning Star's eyes. "Sad. Why?"

Morning Star moaned and Julianne had never seen such grief line another person's face. She shook her head at Morning Star. "I'm sorry. You don't have to tell me."

But Morning Star seemed compelled to share. She pointed to Jonathan, then pointed to her belly. Then she reached down for a handful of dirt and let it gently filter into the wind. Julianne felt a wretchedness of mind she'd never felt before. Morning Star had given birth to a baby and it had died. That's why she had milk to feed Jonathan. Tears blinded her as she reached uncertainly for her new friend, clasping her in a tight hug. Morning Star wept aloud, rocking back and forth in Julianne's embrace. Carried away by her own response she failed to notice the arrival of Morning Star's husband till he cleared his throat. Morning Star ran to him and he wiped the tears off her face. He handed her something and she turned and held it out to Julianne. It was a waterskin filled with a liquid. She pointed at Jonathan then smiled sadly. She walked away with the brave.

They parted as friends, but as Julianne thought back over their visit she felt she'd lost respect in Morning Star's eyes. She instinctively knew her new friend would never show anything other than devotion to her husband, yet Julianne had already dishonored her marriage vows with lies that seemed only to multiply.

Julianne still felt uncomfortable keeping the secret from Caleb, but she would soon have enough money to pay him back, and then could reveal what she'd been doing. If at that time Caleb forbade her from taking trips to the river alone, she would bend to his will.

Until then, she felt her only option was for Maggie to continue to drop off the laundry two or three times a week and pick it up every Friday with payment for the work done.

Julianne pulled her thoughts back to the present. She loved the time she spent with Caleb. Her favorite time of the day had not changed. It was still when her husband came home for the night.

Spring slowly turned to summer and the days grew a bit longer. Caleb and Julianne took long walks in the woods after supper. He always showed her something new. But what impressed her most was when he gave her his total attention and shared what he'd done during the day.

It seemed as though once a week he'd bring home something new for her. First, it had been Maybell, the cow. Then he'd brought home a dozen hens and two roosters. Seeds for the gardens were next, both vegetable and flower.

She'd learned her husband was quite good with a knife and wood. He'd made several more nipples for Jonathan, a rocking chair carved with the same markings as the baby's crib and her headboard. But her favorite piece was a box.

Caleb had given it to her a few days ago as a one-month anniversary gift. She loved the ash wood. He'd carved two doves flying with a vine in both their beaks.

Was he trying to tell her that together they could make

a home just as the birds built their nests? A smile touched her lips and she uttered, "I hope so."

She'd learned also that Caleb was a man of God. He read from the Bible every morning upon rising and every evening before going to bed. And sometimes at night Julianne listened to his soft-spoken conversations with his Lord.

She felt foolish for her earlier fears of Caleb. He was nothing like the men of her past. Caleb was strong, handsome, wise and kind.

Her uncle slipped unbidden into her thoughts, gnawing away at her newfound serenity. The one time she'd mentioned him to Caleb, he'd assured her that her uncle could no longer harm her. He promised he'd protect her, and for whatever it was worth, Julianne felt secure in that knowledge. Besides, her uncle knew where she was if he was the one who had intercepted her letter from Sloan. Surely if he were looking for her, he'd have found her by now.

Even if he was trying to find her, she'd changed her name. Living so far from town and even the camp, Julianne felt sure he'd never find her even if he still searched.

She wasn't too worried about Marcus now, either. Caleb had told her that Marcus took a job in town as a saloon bartender. She shuddered at the memory of the evil in that man's eyes.

He was a wicked man. Everything in her being told her to stay far, far away from him. She didn't see where that would be a problem, considering he worked so far away.

Julianne looked down at little Jonathan as he slept in her arms. He had grown quite a bit in the last month. The baby was lucky to have a man like Caleb as his uncle. She carried him to his crib and laid him down.

The entire cabin smelled of the roast duck cooking in the oven. She sniffed appreciatively then looked about her home. Her home. She exhaled a long sigh of contentment. Everything was perfect. Well, almost.

Her gaze moved to the bag of laundry that taunted her from the far wall. *There's your problem*, her conscience accused. Maggie hadn't come by to pick it up yet, and Julianne couldn't stand to look at it anymore. She needed to get it out of sight, out of her home. She'd find a place outside, where it wouldn't constantly remind her of her deceitfulness and where Caleb was sure not to see it.

Julianne ran her index finger over the carving of the wooden box. She felt it fitting to save the money she'd earned from doing the loggers' laundry in the box her husband had made just for her. Once that debt was paid, then the deception would come to an end, and she would be the true wife Caleb deserved. *Lies and sin*, that same little voice of conscience nagged.

She carried the box to the table. Julianne sat down and opened the lid. Her fingers shook as she counted the money. She had washed clothes several times a week for a month now and each man paid her a dollar a week. There were fifteen men, so thanks to Maggie's idea, in a few more weeks, she'd have enough to pay back Caleb. She gave Maggie money to buy her laundry soap and occasionally Maggie picked up items Julianne needed to cook with, but for the most part she had saved every dime. They could use the money to start the apple orchard Caleb dreamed of someday owning. "Won't he be surprised?" She spoke quietly to herself so as not to wake the baby.

From the corner of her eye, the wash taunted and accused. Julianne sighed. The laundry wasn't going to walk outside by itself. Placing both hands firmly on the table, she pushed up out of the chair. She had no intention of permitting a sack of laundry to create such havoc in her life. She scooped up the bag and headed for the front door.

The cow bawled. The sound traveled on the late afternoon air. Julianne propped the bag against the back of the cabin and hurried to the barn.

"Caleb's late again this evening, Maybell. I guess it's just you and me." She looped a rope over the cow's head and pulled her out into the center aisle to milk.

Maybell stood, patiently observing while Julianne got the bucket and stool. Her tail twitched from side to side. Julianne sat down on the stool and began the milking.

Oh, supper was going to be good if the smell that greeted him was anything to go by. His tired senses revived a bit as he entered the cabin. It had been a long day. He looked about the empty house. Disappointment assaulted him. He'd been looking forward to seeing Julianne.

Jonathan woke up with a cry, his movements rocking the cradle at the foot of Julianne's bed. Caleb moved toward it. Julianne seldom let the baby out of her sight.

He figured she was in the barn milking Maybell. It wasn't the first time he'd come home late and found her there. With her outside, he'd have a chance to hold his nephew.

Caleb smiled down at the baby and picked him up. Jonathan immediately stopped crying, his eyes focused on Caleb's face.

Carrying the baby back to the rocker, he bumped the box causing it to fall off the table. Its contents scattered across the kitchen floor, and he gasped at the amount of coins and bills.

"What in the world…?"

Holding the baby in the crook of one arm, he bent to pick up the money. Where had it come from? Doubts about his wife formed with each piece he picked up.

His thoughts winged back to the day she'd arrived at the camp. Sloan had accused her of stealing his money. Had she? Was he holding the stolen money now?

What did he really know about his new wife? Over the past month he'd told her everything there was to know about himself but she hadn't revealed much information at all.

Was Julianne the thief Sloan had made her out to be?

He put the money back into the box. She'd left it out in plain sight. Maybe his wife planned on telling him about it tonight.

Caleb closed the lid on the box and sat in the rocker. It wasn't right. The box had been facing the other way. He stood up and positioned it just the way it had been and then settled back down in the rocker with the baby.

Would she tell him where she'd gotten the money? He prayed she would.

He didn't have long to wait. Julianne brought the bucket of milk through the front door.

Her eyes darted from him to the oak box. Caleb's heart sank as she set the milk on the counter then scooped the box up and carried it into her room.

She chattered as she did so. "How was your day, Caleb? When I left Jonathan was asleep. I hope you didn't find the little tyke crying." She left the bedroom and hurried back to serve the evening meal.

Caleb listened and watched her move about their home. In disbelief, he realized she wasn't going to mention the money. "No, I think I woke him when I came in." He stood to his feet.

Julianne finished setting the table. "Here, I'll take him." She held out her arms for the baby.

"I've got him." Caleb pulled his nephew closer.

Suddenly, he didn't trust her, and the knowledge pained him. He'd thought they were growing closer, but how could he trust her when she revealed nothing of herself to him?

Chapter 11

Over the next few weeks Caleb watched the money grow in the little wooden box, and with it grew distrust of his wife. Where was the money coming from? What did Julianne do to get it?

Didn't she understand the meaning of the box and the carving he'd etched into it? If they were ever to be a real husband and wife, she would have to be honest with him. Why didn't she understand that?

Julianne acted as if nothing was out of the ordinary. She fixed meals, took care of Jonathan and kept their home clean. But could it really be called a home if there were secrets between husband and wife?

Caleb finished dressing and headed downstairs. His gaze landed on Julianne. She stood in a blue calico dress with small blue laces at the front. The blue brought out the sky color in her eyes. He'd never seen the dress before. Where had she gotten it?

"You look handsome this morning."

The compliment took him by surprise. He watched the color fill her cheeks before she turned back to preparing breakfast.

He listened as she hummed happily. Funny, the more the money grew, the happier Julianne became, and the more miserable he felt. They needed to talk about it. Caleb decided that after church he and his wife were going to discuss the contents of that box.

Caleb walked over to where Jonathan played in the crib. The baby smiled up at him happily. He couldn't stop himself from looking toward the box.

The box he wished he'd never made, the box that held the money and filled his heart with doubt.

"Breakfast is ready, Caleb. Would you bring Jonathan with you when you come?"

"Come on, little fella." He scooped up Jonathan into his arms and went to the table.

After he said grace, Julianne asked. "Do you think one apple pie and one peach cobbler will be enough dessert, Caleb?"

"It'll be plenty. Those men will just have to be happy with what they get."

Julianne took Jonathan from him. "I know, but they do so love my pies and cobblers." She sat down with the baby and gave him his bottle. "I should have baked more." They had continued the meal on the grounds every Sunday after church for several reasons. It helped feed those who didn't have enough, and it gave the few women in the settlement a much-needed time of fellowship.

"Why didn't you?"

He watched her study the baby's face and chew on her bottom lip.

"I was busy with the baby and lost track of time."

A frown marred her delicate features. Caleb could tell the lie tasted bitter in her mouth. He wondered what the real reason was for her not baking more. Did it have anything to do with the money?

"He hasn't been fretting like he did in the beginning, right? Seems like he's finally adjusted to the milk."

To his amazement, Julianne flinched at his question and moved restlessly. A warning voice whispered in his head. His misgivings increased by the minute.

They ate in silence. The food tasted like sawdust in his mouth. He finished the meal then picked up his Bible and led his little family to church.

Julianne hated the silence that surrounded her and Caleb. She hated lying to him. But she hadn't known what to say. It was no excuse, and she knew it. Lying was wrong no matter the reason.

But how could she tell him Jonathan's tummy accepted Morning Star's milk without telling him how and where she met the Indian woman and why she accepted the skin bag of milk each time they washed together?

Caleb helped her down from the buggy when they got to the church. She held his gaze as he set her down on the hard ground. His eyes begged her to tell him the truth but she couldn't.

"I'd think you two would have stopped staring into each other's eyes by now." Maggie stood behind them.

Julianne sighed unhappily when Caleb pulled his gaze from her and smiled at the older woman.

"Now, Maggie. She's my wife, and I can stare at her

all day, if I've a mind to." He turned to the wagon and reached for his Bible and Jonathan's bag.

"Well, I guess you can at that." Maggie hugged Julianne. "That pretty blue sure makes the color in your eyes pop out."

"Thank you, Maggie." Julianne fussed with Jonathan's blankets as she followed the older woman into the church.

She couldn't stop the grin no matter how hard she tried. A vision of her eyes popping out and rolling around in the dirt caused her to chuckle out loud.

The laugh caught in her throat when Caleb dropped his arm from around her shoulder and greeted the pastor. "Good Morning, Reverend. What do you have in store for us today?"

"I'll be teaching on the Garden of Eden and how one lie caused the fall of mankind, and how the sin of omission is still a lie." The preacher shook Caleb's hand.

"Sounds like a good sermon. We better hurry and get a seat." Caleb placed his hand in the center of Julianne's back and gently helped her into the church.

She was thankful for his support. She wasn't sure her feet would have moved forward if not for him.

Lying.

Why lying?

Did the pastor know of her sin? Was it possible?

Did everyone know she had lied to her husband? Not just about washing the men's clothes, but also the fact that in the beginning her intentions were purely selfish. She hadn't cared that Caleb had an infant to raise—she had planned to use the money she made to buy her freedom from marriage to him. Wasn't lying by omission still as bad as an outright lie? Though now she planned to help him grow the orchard, did everyone suspect the money had been her escape route? She couldn't tell Caleb about Morning Star unless she told him about washing the men's clothes. What a tangled web of lies. And now she suspected everyone knew she had lied to her husband. Was still lying to him.

The service started with songs and prayer. Julianne tried to fill her mind with the joy of singing. But then the preacher entered the pulpit and told everyone to turn in their Bibles to Genesis three verse four. Her palms turned sweaty, and her heartbeat quickened.

He read the scripture aloud for those who didn't have Bibles. "And the serpent said unto the woman, Ye shall not surely die."

Julianne stared down at Jonathan. The top of her head felt on fire. Was the preacher looking at her? Was everyone looking at her?

The preacher continued. "Because of that one lie, Eve disobeyed God. She and her mate, Adam, fell from God's grace."

His voice continued on. Julianne tried to think of something else. She knew she was lying to her husband. She didn't need to be reminded of it by a preacher. Sorrow, deep and painful, tore at her heart.

Jonathan began to fuss. Julianne took that moment to escape. She scooped up the baby and grabbed his bag. Her feet led her outside to the big oak tree.

Tears streamed down her face.

When had she started crying? Had anyone seen the tears?

She glanced over her shoulder back to the church. No one had followed her so she sank down at the base of the large pine tree.

Julianne changed Jonathan's diaper and began to talk to God. Her hands did the work while her heart did the talking.

"Lord, I didn't think this lie would hurt Caleb. I never wanted to do that. Father, please forgive me. Forgive me of all my sins and come live in my heart so that I won't do it again." A peace like no other filled her. She savored the feeling of being wrapped in warm loving arms. "Caleb said you love me so much you sent your son to die for me. I believe him, and I realize now that the only way he will ever believe me is if I stop lying to him. I'll tell Caleb everything. I don't know how, but I will. I promise."

She wiped the tears from her face and gathered the baby close. Julianne looked up into the sky that peeked through the many trees.

"I'll tell Caleb after lunch. Lord, please let him forgive me, too."

The sound of male voices singing "Bringing in the Sheaves" carried out the church doors. Julianne slipped back inside. Everyone was standing, so she took her place beside Caleb.

He leaned over and whispered. "Is the baby okay?"

Julianne tucked her hand into his. "He's fine. Everything is fine." She rocked Jonathan in time with the beat of the song.

For the first time in her life, she felt free. The song ended and Julianne handed Jonathan to Caleb. She quickly gathered their things and joined the loggers and the few families as they made their way out of the small church.

She hurried to help the other women set the food on the tables for the picnic. Julianne wanted to tell Caleb of her new commitment to God and to confess her lie to him so they could go back to being comfortable with each other. He hadn't said anything, but Julianne sensed he knew she was hiding something from him.

"You're awful chipper." Maggie commented, setting a large potato salad on the table.

Julianne felt the older woman studying her face. She tried to hide her newfound joy from her friend. Caleb should be the first one to be told.

"You've changed. There's a sparkle in your eyes that weren't there this morning." Maggie moved in front of her.

Julianne was forced to look the older woman in the eye. She opened her mouth to deny the truth of Maggie's words and then stopped. Her lying days were over.

"I really want to tell Caleb first, Maggie." She whispered, leaning toward her friend.

Maggie clapped her hands with joy drawing attention to them. "You're with a wee one, aren't you?" She grabbed Julianne and hugged her to her breast.

Over Maggie's shoulder Julianne watched as Caleb's face turned as white as new-fallen snow.

One of the men from the sawmill burst into the churchyard, yelling, "We need every man on the west side. A fire is blazin' and it's headed this way!"

His shout drew everyone's attention from Julianne, except Caleb's.

Maggie ran to where Caleb and the men stood. "I'll come and help."

Caleb handed Jonathan to her. "No, Maggie we need you here to send food and water up to us. Would you see my family gets home okay?"

"You know I will."

Chapter 12

Julianne watched Caleb leave with the men. She had to explain it to him. Surely, he didn't really think she was with child. What must he be thinking?

She found herself silently praying. *Lord, what a mess this is. Please comfort my husband and keep him safe as he fights the fire.*

Maggie carried Jonathan back to Julianne. "I'm sorry. I wish it had been a better time to tell Caleb about the babe."

"I'm not having a baby, Maggie." Julianne took Jonathan.

"Oh, well." Concern filled her voice. "I'm pretty sure Caleb thinks you are. Maybe you are and just don't know it yet." Maggie offered as she began filling a plate with food. "But since you don't know fer sure, it will be a simple thing to straighten out when he gets home. Who knows, maybe he'll think about it and decide he likes the idea."

Julianne felt tears prick her eyes. She refused to cry. Maggie had no way of knowing their marriage wasn't real or of the anguish she had just caused Caleb.

She followed Maggie to one of the many trees that surrounded the churchyard. Maggie spread out an old blanket, and the two women sank down on it to eat lunch.

Jonathan fell asleep to Julianne's gentle rocking. She lay him down on the blanket beside her and looked about.

Two women with small children sat together talking in soft whispers. Julianne couldn't hear what they were saying but was pretty sure they were voicing their concern for their husbands. Another woman sat by herself. She held a new baby to her breast and sang "Amazing Grace" in a quiet, soothing way.

"Well, if you weren't happy 'cause you're with child, what put that new sparkle in your eyes?" Maggie took a bite of fried chicken.

Julianne thought of the moments she'd spent in the presence of the Lord. She really wanted to tell someone and since Caleb wasn't there…why not tell Maggie?

"Maggie, I opened my heart to Jesus this morning." The words came out a whisper.

"Well, glory be! It's about time." Maggie set her plate to the side and hugged Julianne.

Surrounded in the happiness of her friend, Julianne poured her heart out. "All these months I've been afraid my uncle would come and snatch me away. Maggie, it was as if God took that fear away." She hesitated, "Don't get me wrong. I'm still scared he'll come, but now I know God will protect me."

Maggie took both Julianne's hands in hers and searched

her face. "This uncle, he's the reason you been doing laundry and making money? If he came, were you going to leave Caleb and that baby behind and just keep running?"

"Oh, no, I'd never even thought of that. I wanted to repay Caleb. He's been talking about starting an apple orchard, but we don't have enough money to buy the seedlings right now. I'm going to give him the money." Julianne stared at her friend. She saw the doubt in Maggie's eyes.

"You still think I took Sloan's money don't you?"

Maggie dropped Julianne's hands and picked her plate back up. "It don't matter none."

Julianne's heart constricted. It felt as if Maggie had taken a knife and twisted it. It did matter. If Maggie still doubted her, did Caleb? She wasn't sure.

"I'm going home." Julianne stood. She picked up Jonathan and her plate of untouched food.

Maggie jumped to her feet. "I'm going with you. I promised that man of yours I would keep an eye on you while he was gone."

Julianne felt hurt turn to anger as it welled up and spilled over. She turned to the older woman. "I don't need a babysitter, Maggie. Jonathan and I are going home alone."

She didn't give Maggie time to respond. Julianne put Jonathan's things into their wagon and laid the baby down on the floor then climbed up. The blue sheet slipped easily over her head. Julianne picked up the baby and gently laid him in the folds. Then, she took the reins in her hands and turned the animals toward home.

Tears filled her eyes. How was it that everyone still thought she was a thief? Even after all these weeks, they still condemned her for a crime she hadn't committed. Julianne thought they'd grown to know and love her. Now she realized it was all just an illusion.

Julianne heard a horse following her. She was sure it was Maggie. Maggie was a woman of her word. It gave her some comfort to know her friend cared some for her, even if she didn't trust her.

The next morning Julianne rose with a headache. She wasn't sure if the headache was from worrying about Caleb fighting the fire all night, or if it was from the tears she'd cried when he hadn't come home. "Probably both," she told Jonathan, taking him from the crib. Her nerves were frayed from all the soul-searching she'd done. Had Caleb been injured in the fire or simply been fed up with his wife's lies?

"You and I are going to the river today. I'm going to do this last basket of laundry, and then I'm telling Maggie I'm out of the clothes-washing business." She continued to talk to the baby as she prepared.

"Things are going to change around here. I've had a lot of time to think about this mess, and I've decided to tell Caleb everything." *If I get the chance.*

Jonathan cooed up at her as she gently slipped him into her sling. "I know what you're thinking. But I have to tell him that my uncle must have taken Sloan's money. I couldn't tell him before because I didn't want anyone to know I was running away from home. Someone might have felt compelled to send word to my uncle. Now I need Caleb to know the truth and to trust me. If we are to be a real family, there should be nothing between us." She lifted the basket and closed the cabin door.

Heading down to the river, she continued with her

conversation. "I also told God I would tell Caleb about our little jaunts down here." The baby smiled up at her.

"Oh, you like the sound of that do you?" She entered the clearing and looked up into the clear blue sky. "I just hope he doesn't get too upset with me."

Julianne set down the laundry and hugged the baby to her for several long moments. Thoughts of Caleb fighting the fire troubled her. She decided to pray for him.

But how did one pray? Really pray?

She thought back to the many nights that Caleb had prayed for them both before going to bed each evening. His prayers had sounded like he was talking to someone right there in the room with them. Julianne took a deep breath and began.

"Lord, please watch over Caleb and protect him while he fights the fire." Julianne opened her eyes and stared down at Jonathan. His sleepy eyes reassured her.

Feeling as if someone were watching her, Julianne looked over her shoulder. The bush behind her moved ever so slightly.

Julianne saw Morning Star's doeskin dress. She smiled and opened her mouth to greet her friend.

The Indian woman shook her head *no* and raised a finger to her lips. Her dark eyes darted toward the tree line and she repeated her earlier actions.

What was wrong with her? Morning Star had never hidden before. The two women always worked fast and then spent several hours sitting on the bank with their feet in the river playing with the baby.

Julianne looked about her and listened. For the first time, she noticed the silence. The birds weren't singing. When she looked back to where her friend had stood, no one was there.

Her stomach rolled. Something was terribly wrong. She turned to pick up the laundry.

"Well, well. Look what I found."

The voice came from behind her. Julianne froze. She felt icy fingers of fear trickle down her neck. Every hair seemed to stand on end as his name ricocheted off the walls of her mind.

Marcus.

Had he seen Jonathan? She lifted the sling over her head and wrapped the sheet around the sleeping baby. *Lord, please don't let him hurt Jonathan.*

"What'sa matter, Julianne? Don't you recognize me?" The words were playful, but the meaning was not.

Her throat closed with a terror she'd never known before. Her mouth went dry. She heard his boots crush the gravel as he came closer.

Julianne prayed he wouldn't hear the fear in her voice. "Hello, Marcus." She laid the baby in the basket and turned to face her enemy. Julianne purposely moved away from the basket, praying he'd not pay attention to the precious bundle she'd just deposited inside.

"'Hello, Marcus'?" His voice mocked her. "That's all you have to say? 'Hello, Marcus'?"

Morning Star moved silently behind him. She knelt to pick up a large rock.

Marcus grabbed Julianne by the throat. His fingers closed, shutting off her air. Julianne's arms flailed through the air, and she clawed at his face.

Her vision blurred as she vainly tried to suck in air. Morning Star melted back into the forest. No help there. She swatted at Marcus, her strength waning.

"Marcus! I'm not paying you to kill her."

Her uncle's familiar voice seemed to come from a

great distance away. The vise around her neck released and she staggered. Julianne would have fallen, but Marcus jerked her forward and pinned her back to his chest with one easy sweep.

Julianne gasped for breath. When she raised her head all the air she'd pulled into her lungs moments before burst back out in a whoosh.

"Didn't expect to see me did you, Julie girl?"

Chapter 13

Caleb made his way home. His arms ached, his back hurt, and his heart felt as if it had been stomped on and thrown to the dogs. For two days, as he fought the flames, the thought of Julianne being with another man tore him apart.

He couldn't bring himself to believe she had been unfaithful. Maybe she'd been pregnant when they got married and hadn't known it.

Had she been married before? Was she carrying a baby that was conceived before she came to the territory? It was possible. After all, what did he know about her life before she'd come here?

The horse picked up the pace as it neared the cabin. Caleb slumped deeper into the saddle. The canopy of branches further darkened his mood as he passed under them.

Why hadn't she told him? Did she think he would

throw her out? Could it be she still didn't trust him? The questions troubled Caleb.

Well, his wife would find out that she could trust him. He loved her and had promised to protect her, in sickness and in health. Caleb sat up straighter in the saddle.

He urged the horse toward home. It was time he and Julianne put all their doubts and fears behind them and settled a few things. It was time he told her he loved her.

Caleb stopped the horse.

He loved her.

The thought took him by surprise. But, it was true. Caleb Hansen was in love with his wife. Not the mushy kind of love his sister had talked about before she'd married, but the deep, soul-searching kind.

A tug on the reins reminded him of the horse's impatience to be home. He gave the anxious animal its head and soon was speeding down the path towards his own little haven.

As the horse entered the clearing, Caleb felt that something wasn't right. It was as if the thought came from deep within him. He slowed the horse to a walk.

The little wooden structure rested snugly against the mountain. But, there was no smoke drifting into the morning mist from the chimney and it looked cold and vacant instead of warm and inviting.

Caleb turned the horse back into the tree line and circled the house. Nothing moved. He approached the barn from behind. The horse neighed. A soft moo answered from inside the barn.

He slid to the ground, tied the reins loosely to the saddle horn and let the horse go. His body blending into the shadows of the barn, Caleb eased his way toward the cabin. No sound came from within as he pressed his back against the wall.

Dread and unease threatened to overwhelm his good sense. He crept around to the front of the cabin and slipped inside the unbarred door.

The stillness grated on his nerves. He moved through the lower half of his home. Julianne and the baby were gone. Caleb hurried up the stairs. A quick glance about showed no signs of his family.

He descended the stairs two at a time. His tired, confused mind chanted. *She's gone. Julianne has taken the baby and left you.*

Caleb sank into the rocker. Why had she left? Was it because he knew about her unborn child? Didn't she know by now how he felt about her? He hung his head. How could she? He'd never told her.

Where would she have gone? And did she have enough money to get there? His head came up. *The money.* Had she finally acquired enough to leave?

He stood and made his way to the box he'd crafted for her. Caleb ran his dirty hand over the surface of the wood. An ache ran through his chest as he opened the lid.

He'd expected the box to be empty but the money was still there. "What is going on here?" His voice echoed in the empty room.

Once more, the thought that things weren't right struck him. The only way to get answers was to return to the logging camp and find Maggie. Maybe she would know where Julianne was.

He smiled. Why hadn't he thought of that before? Julianne and Jonathan were probably staying with Maggie until he got home.

Caleb closed the box and hurried out to the barn. The

horse had nosed his way inside and stood in the corner munching on hay. He stepped up to the animal and stuck his foot into the stirrup. Something moved in the stall on the opposite side of the horse. Caleb froze and his heart hammered in his chest.

As he reprimanded himself a young Indian woman materialized out of the shadows. She held a small blue bundle tightly against her chest. Dirty tearstains marred her light brown cheeks.

Caleb recognized the blue sheet Julianne used to hold Jonathan. His foot dropped from the stirrup and the dull ache of foreboding became so acute it was a physical pain. He pushed the horse out of the way and stumbled toward her.

"Give him to me." She released the baby into his arms, her shoulders heaving, a hiccupped sob escaping as she stepped away from him.

Caleb unwrapped the baby and checked that his little body was unharmed. Jonathan slept contently, happily unaware of the fear welling in Caleb's heart.

"Where is Julianne?" His throat was so tight his voice came out a whisper.

"Julianne." The cry erupted from her lips and she ran.

Caleb chased her out of the barn. He couldn't let her escape. He'd seen the fear in her eyes, and she was his only link to Julianne.

His boots thundered down the path leading to the river as he ran after the young woman. Julianne would never have willingly given up the baby. Had the Indian woman's tribe taken Julianne captive? Caleb pushed the troublesome thought aside. The tribes in this area were peaceful people.

Jonathan awoke with a scared little whimper.

Caleb had no time to comfort the baby as he ran. He couldn't risk the chance that the woman would hide from him. The natives were experts at disappearing when they wanted or needed to. He would not give up till this woman told him where Julianne was!

Julianne lay curled in a tight ball on her side. Her hands and feet were tied together in front of her. A dirty rag had been stuffed into her mouth, and another rag had been tied around her head to hold the gag in place.

She'd almost escaped once, but that had been before her uncle caught her using her teeth to untie the knots.

How long was he going to keep her here? The run-down shack didn't keep out the cold, the bugs or the snakes. Julianne shivered with chill and fatigue. The nerves in her hands and feet were numb. Her muscles screamed from the strain of the awkward position in which she lay. Her eyes burned from sleeplessness.

She'd only seen her uncle twice since they'd dumped her here. The first time had been when she'd tried to escape, and he'd caught her. The second had been last night, when he'd come and told Marcus he had a little job for him to do and both men had left.

Her latest visitor was another skunk. Of the animal variety this time. It nosed its way about the dirty cabin. Julianne didn't move. The last thing she wanted was to get sprayed by the nasty animal. Black eyes studied her warily. She held her breath, watching, till finally it lost interest in her. Its black-and-white body moved around the room with a purpose. The skunk finished its search and sashayed out the broken door.

Julianne relaxed and closed her eyes. Her whole body was engulfed in weariness and despair. The last two nights had been cold, and rats and who knew what else moving about in the darkness had kept her awake.

The sound of her uncle, Edmond Bartholomew III, clapping his hands in pleasure woke her up. "Come, come. Are you going to spend this glorious day sleeping?"

Julianne glared at him from where she lay.

"Marcus, untie her," her uncle ordered.

The big lumberjack stepped through the door and knelt down beside her. He pulled his knife from his boot and waved it in her face.

"Stop tormenting her, and do as I say," her uncle barked, pulling a large tree stump farther into the room.

Marcus slid the knife through the ropes at her feet. He moved the knife to her hands and let the cold blade prick into her skin before slicing the ropes. She felt his breath on her face as he untied the gag, but she refused to give him the satisfaction of looking at him.

Her legs ached and her hands throbbed as the blood returned feeling to her limbs. It took Julianne several moments to straighten her legs. She fought back tears of frustration.

"You, my dear, will return with me on the next voyage home. Your Aunt Mary and the kids have missed you something awful." He pulled the stump toward her.

Julianne struggled to her feet. "I'm not going anywhere, Uncle Edmond. I have a husband and a home here. You can't make me go."

Swifter than she expected, he slapped her hard across the mouth. "Who do you think you are? I am your guardian, and I say you are coming home with me!"

"I'm Caleb Hansen's wife." Julianne wiped the blood from her lips. For the first time since her parents' accident, Julianne felt loved and secure. "He will come for me."

Her uncle laughed harshly, "Oh, I don't think so. You see…" he paused and waited for Julianne to give him her full attention "…by now you are a widow."

Shock siphoned the blood from her face. She stood there, blank, amazed and very shaken, too stunned to even cry.

Then a small sliver of doubt curled its way into her mind. Was it true? Could Caleb really be dead? Or, was this just another of her Uncle Edmond's cruel attempts to make her do as he wanted? A flicker of something— she wasn't sure what—stirred inside her heart. She loved Caleb. Surely if he were dead her heart would grieve.

Torn by conflicting emotions, she denied his words. "I don't believe you."

"Sit, child. You're tired." Her uncle indicated the large stump.

Julianne sank onto the hard surface. In her heart, she prayed he was lying. Surely God wouldn't let this happen to them. She had been so close to telling Caleb the truth, finally freeing herself to love him with nothing standing between.

"Marcus, tell Mrs. Hansen about her husband's untimely death." Edmond walked over to the doorway. He lit a cigar and blew smoke out the door.

She turned her weary gaze from her uncle. What vile things would Marcus make up to convince her Caleb was dead? Julianne watched an evil grin creep across the man's face.

He stooped down in front of her and twirled the knife in his hands. "Oh, he's dead, all right. I personally watched his body float down the river." Hard eyes bored into her.

Fear gnawed away at her fragile belief that Caleb was still alive.

"Of course, he had a little help getting into the river." Hatred radiated from the man as he laughed. His dancing eyes seemed to delight in her misery.

The laughter stopped as quickly as it started. "Caleb is dead. My ax found its way into the small of his back. Then it was an easy matter to shove him into the river."

Julianne shook her head. It couldn't be true. Her heart ached, and her mouth went dry. She forced herself to listen to Marcus's account of what had befallen her husband, analyzing each word for clues.

"With the fire and all going on, no one is going to miss either of you for days." He sneered in her face.

Fresh tears worked their way down Julianne's face. Her chest felt tight. Her breathing became shallow and forced. *Let the darkness take you*, her mind shouted. She heaved to breathe. Black circles swam before her eyes, and she knew she would faint any moment.

Marcus leaned close to her ear and whispered. "Don't think I've forgotten I owe you, too." He reached a hand forward and rubbed his thumb across her swollen, cracked lips.

From deep in her center, Julianne fought the instinct to surrender. If she passed out, who knew what these depraved men would do to her? She shook her head, leaning forward, head between her knees.

Edmond flicked the remainder of the cigar out the door. "Marcus! Leave her be!"

The logger grabbed Julianne's hair and pulled her head up. He stared into her eyes. He made as if to kiss her, pressing his mouth alongside her cheekbone. "Don't expect your uncle to protect you forever." Then he stepped away from her.

"Sorry, boss." Marcus's voice sounded contrite but his eyes remained cold as stone as they bored into Julianne, daring her to voice what he'd just whispered to her.

Julianne stared up at him. What did he plan to do? Had he really killed Caleb? And what about Jonathan? If Caleb was dead, where was their son?

She forced herself to look away from the man who claimed to have murdered the only man who'd ever cared for her. Julianne focused her gaze on her uncle. "I won't go."

"Oh, I think you will." Edmond pulled another stump across the room. His breath mingled with hers as he sat down in front of her. He grabbed both her hands and held them tightly together.

His narrow eyes bored into hers. "Marcus, how far is it to that Indian village?"

Marcus moved to stand behind Edmond. "'Bout a half day's ride from here, boss. Want me ta pay them a visit?" He twirled the knife and smiled wickedly at Julianne over her uncle's shoulder.

Now what would he threaten her with? Julianne glanced back and forth between the two men. She finally decided that since Edmond was the boss, he would be the one to tell her what their next move would be.

"What do you think, Julie girl? Should I send Marcus after the baby?"

Icy fear twisted around her heart. They knew about Jonathan. Morning Star had taken him, just as Julianne had known she would. *Thank you, God.* Right on the trail of her relief-filled prayer, she hesitated, blinking with bafflement. How did her uncle know she had a baby? Marcus of course, but how did they know Morning Star had him?

Her heart beat faster, and her hands grew clammy in his. Would he do such a thing? Julianne looked into her uncle's cold gray eyes, and for the first time in her life, she knew her uncle was capable of murder. When had he become this monster? And why?

Chapter 14

The young Indian woman stopped at the river's edge and pointed to the ground.

Caleb came to an abrupt stop. He shuffled Jonathan around in his arms and stared at the ground where she pointed.

By the markings in the dirt Caleb knew instantly there had been a fight here. What did that have to do with Julianne? His gaze moved to the woman.

She pointed again, "Julianne." Her eyes entreated him to understand what her language could not tell him.

"Who are you?" He didn't wait for her reply. He knelt and placed a hand on the prints, his gaze scanning the torn-up earth. Two pairs of boot tracks marred the ground.

"Morning Star."

"Were there two men, Morning Star?" Caleb looked up at her. He prayed she would understand and tell him what happened.

Her head tilted sideways and her forehead furrowed. He held up his hand and two fingers then pointed at the footprints in the sand.

Morning Star's forehead cleared and she nodded quickly. She raised her hand high, signaling a tall person and then made a circle with her arms that he assumed represented a heavier person. She moved toward him. Keeping her eyes lowered, she touched his chest.

"I sure hope you are trying to tell me they are men like me." Caleb removed her hand from his chest and again examined the tracks. His heart lurched. One set of smaller footprints could be detected in the sand.

Deep down he knew they were Julianne's. He studied the direction they had gone. She'd put up quite a fight. He found deep indentations in the sand where she'd dug in her heels.

Caleb ignored Morning Star as she began speaking rapidly in her own language.

"She says two men came and stole your woman."

Caleb straightened so quickly he stumbled. An Indian man stood beside Morning Star.

He wanted to kick himself. He'd been studying the tracks, worrying about Julianne, and hadn't paid attention to his surroundings. That was the second mistake in one day. In the wild, that was a good way to get killed. Morning Star spoke once more to the man. She said Caleb's name and pointed to him and then to Jonathan.

"My woman says you are friend, Caleb. I am Runs Swiftly." He stepped forward and gasped Caleb's forearm. After several long seconds, he dropped Caleb's arm and crossed his over his chest.

"Does Morning Star know where they took Julianne?"

Caleb asked. While Morning Star talked to her husband, Caleb bent once more to study the tracks.

Who had her and why? Once more the woman pointed into the woods then looked at Caleb. "They took her two sunsets past." The man shifted as if worried. "Caleb is a good tracker?"

Two days ago? The words sank into Caleb's heart. They could be anywhere by now. The trail was cold and in truth, Caleb wasn't sure whether he could track them or not.

"I've never tracked men, only animals. I'm not sure..." When he'd tracked animals, there had been no urgency or danger. But, for Julianne, he would try.

A firm hand landed roughly on his shoulder. "Runs Swiftly is a good tracker. We will find your woman, Caleb."

Caleb breathed a quick prayer of thanks heavenward for sending Runs Swiftly to him in his time of need. "Thank you. When do we leave?"

Runs Swiftly turned to Morning Star. He spoke quickly, motioning to the baby and then back to her.

"Morning Star and your woman are sisters." The Indian seemed to search his mind for the correct words. "Friends." He stood tall and powerful, like a towering spruce. "Morning Star will care for the papoose till we find your woman."

Indecision ate at Caleb's confidence. For all he knew, this was a trap. His instincts told him he was running out of time but the voice of reason insisted he take Jonathan to Maggie's and round up some of the men to help him.

Then, he looked at the tear tracks on Morning Star's face and remembered how lovingly she'd handed the baby to him back at the barn. If what she said was true,

Morning Star had taken care of Jonathan for two days while she'd waited for his return.

"Lord, I need you," he whispered, running a hand through his hair. He looked down at the babe sucking on his thumb and made his decision. He placed a kiss on Jonathan's forehead and handed him to Morning Star.

Morning Star enfolded Jonathan in her arms and caressed his tiny head with her cheek. She came closer to Caleb and said something he did not understand then ran into the woods before he could stop her.

Caleb started after her but Runs Swiftly placed a firm hand on his shoulder. "Morning Star is going to our village. She will send others to follow the trail."

"I want my son back, Runs Swiftly." Caleb had lost Julianne he didn't plan on loosing Jonathan too.

Runs Swiftly nodded. "Morning Star will take care of your son until you bring his mother home."

Julianne stumbled over a root that protruded out of the ground. Her hands took the worst of the fall. She sat up and dusted them off on her skirt.

Her uncle stopped and looked down at her. His face turned purple with rage. "Enough of this stalling, Julie girl."

"I tripped." She studied her bruised and bleeding palms.

He stomped back to where she sat on the ground. His rough hands grabbed her and jerked her to her feet. His boot caught the hem of her dress and it ripped. "You're stalling. We both know it."

Julianne didn't argue with him. She took a deep breath and wiped her hands on the ruined dress. "Uncle Edmond, are we lost?"

His gray gaze darted around the dense woods. "Of course I'm not lost." He pulled her along behind him, not caring that briars scratched her legs and tree limbs caught her cheek more than once.

The only parts of the forest she'd been in had been the path to the creek where she washed clothes and small sections where Caleb had cleared the cedar and pine to make room for their future apple orchard. They weren't on a path now, and the trees were so close she felt she might just suffocate.

Not a ray of sunshine filtered through, making it difficult to guess the time of day. The underbrush had gotten worse and sharp roots stubbed her toes. How much longer would her uncle deny being lost and stop to get his bearings?

"Can we rest, please? I'm tired."

He continued on as if she hadn't spoken. Try though she may, she couldn't figure out why they were going away from the ocean. If he planned to make a return voyage, shouldn't they be near the water's edge, buying passage on one of the ships?

Julianne decided to use his ego against him. "Uncle Edmond, I'm not as used to the woods as you are. You're a skilled woodsman. Can we please stop for a short break? I really am tired." She prayed her voice sounded weak and submissive.

Edmond stopped his rapid walk and stood a little taller. "Well, I guess we could rest a few minutes. That should give Marcus time to catch up with us."

Julianne sat down under a tree, thankful her ruse had worked. Surely by now, Morning Star had told someone of her plight. Or maybe Maggie would send help. She refused to give up the idea that someone was looking for her.

If Caleb knew, Julianne was certain he would come for her. She wasn't sure when she decided that he was alive; she simply knew she could not survive without him.

"I wonder where Marcus is at." Edmond looked around the area in which they had stopped.

Julianne didn't want to think about Marcus. He'd left right after a cold breakfast of hard biscuits and she hoped he never caught up with them again.

Under her lashes Julianne watched her uncle turn in a circle. She lowered her head to hide the satisfaction she felt over their situation. They were lost.

"Uncle, how did you meet up with Marcus in the first place?" If she could get him to talk maybe she could find a chink in his armor, a weakening in the mean stance he had demonstrated toward her so far. In the last years she'd lived with him, he had treated her unkindly, but he had never shown such open animosity.

"Oh, girly. A few pointed questions here and there and a person can turn up all kinds of information. A smile covered his face. "In looking for Sloan, your first intended, I found Marcus. And, I did it the very first day I arrived in Seattle. Bartenders know everything that's going on. And one who's been scorned is especially willing to tell what he knows.

"At first he was wary of me, but after a few drinks Marcus spewed forth all the hatred he felt for Julianne Maxwell and Caleb Hansen." He turned and faced Julianne. His gaze studied her for several minutes before he added. "A man who hates that badly can be talked into anything if the price is right." He shrugged matter-of-factly.

Julianne wondered just what Marcus had been talked into. She closed her eyes and silently prayed that the

Lord would hurry and deliver her before the evil man returned to them.

"Don't go to sleep. We need to get going." He barked the command.

"I won't, Uncle. Can't we stay for just a few minutes longer?" Julianne opened her eyes, pulled off her shoe and rubbed her foot.

From the corner of her eye, she watched Edmond ease his cumbersome body under a tall evergreen tree. He closed his eyes and leaned his head back against the trunk. "Don't think about running away, Julie girl."

"I won't, Uncle. I'm too tired to run." Julianne silently thanked God she didn't have to lie. Her back ached between her shoulder blades and her legs burned with fatigue.

The birds chirped happily overhead. In the cool of the trees, Edmond relaxed. Soon his soft snores reached Julianne's ears.

She watched him for several minutes and then eased to her feet. His snores continued uninterrupted. She moved as quietly as the leaves on the ground would allow.

When she was several feet away from him, Julianne turned to run. She prayed the Lord would forgive her for lying to her uncle. Surely her God would understand. Julianne ran right into Marcus's firm chest. He caught her up in one strong arm.

Julianne kicked and screamed as he tried to kiss her.

Edmond hurried to them. "Let her go!" He ordered breathlessly.

For the first time in days, Julianne was glad to hear her uncle's voice. She continued to fight Marcus, until he shoved her hard and her bottom hit the ground with a thud.

Julianne looked up just as her uncle's hand came down across the top of her head. Pain shot through her left eye. She felt as if her head might explode. She scooted backward out of the line of fire.

"Boss, we can't take her to town if she's all beat up." Marcus stood off to the side.

To town? Which town? They were traveling away from Seattle. And why would they take her to town? Questions surged through Julianne's mind even as she cringed, expecting another slap.

A baby's cry split the air.

Julianne's head shot up. She ignored the pain in her eye. Where had the sound come from? Her gaze zeroed in on Marcus.

He scooped up a bundle from the ground and held it out to his side. An evil grin touched his lips but not his eyes. "I got it, boss."

Julianne watched her uncle's face change from rage to surprised pleasure. With fearful clarity, understanding dawned. Edmond had sent Marcus after Jonathan. An even more terrifying realization washed over her. They were going to use the baby against her.

"No." The whisper tore from her parched throat.

Edmond took the baby from Marcus. He unfolded the blanket from the child's face. "Oh, he's a cute one, Julie girl."

She sat up and watched as her uncle cooed down at the infant. She couldn't see Jonathan from where she sat on the ground. Her throat closed. *Oh Lord, how could this have happened?* "Can I see him, please?" Julianne hated begging but knew it was the only way her uncle would listen to her.

He walked within reaching distance of her. "I'm

not an unreasonable man, Julie. All I want you to do is come home with no more trouble. I'll even let you keep the brat." Edmond stared down at the baby. A frown marred his face as he turned that gaze on her, one eyebrow raised.

"I'll go, just please let me have my baby." Julianne scooted along the ground, inching closer to her uncle.

He moved farther away, taunting her. "If I let you keep him, will you come home with no more of this nonsense?" His eyes searched her face.

Julianne nodded. She'd do anything to keep Jonathan safe.

"I guess we could say I adopted him." Edmond's hand rubbed the blanket over the baby's back.

Lord, please let me have Jonathan. Don't let them hurt him, Julianne prayed silently. Her gaze moved to Marcus, and she stiffened with shock. He stared at her uncle with something akin to murder in his eyes.

"I don't care what we do with it, boss. But, we need to get moving. It's gonna be dark soon." Marcus pushed away from the tree he'd been leaning against and walked off into the woods.

Julianne watched her uncle stiffen, and when he turned to face her, his face seemed pale. Was he afraid of Marcus? What was going on between the two of them? This situation had the potential to become even more dangerous. She had to protect Jonathan, even if it cost her life.

Her uncle rewrapped the baby, and then placed him gently into her arms. "Come on, girl."

Julianne cuddled the baby against her chest. Tears of sorrow flowed down her cheeks as her thoughts clarified.

Jonathan was here with her, and that could only mean one thing. Marcus had killed Morning Star to get him.

Edmond jerked her to her feet. "Keep up or I'll bash the brat's head against one of these trees. Do you hear me, Julie?"

Julianne nodded. She didn't take time to inspect Jonathan. It was enough to know he was alive and in her arms. As long as he was with her, he would be safe. She followed her uncle into the woods and rocked the baby until she herself no longer cried.

Chapter 15

Runs Swiftly slowly approached the run-down shack. He motioned for Caleb to follow. No sound came from within.

Caleb entered first. The darkness inside blinded him. He pressed his body against the wall and listened.

"They are gone from this place, my friend." Runs Swiftly moved about the room. He picked up some discarded rope and held it out to Caleb.

Caleb took the rope and studied it. The thought of Julianne being tied made his stomach turn. He tossed the braided cord to the ground. "How long do you think they have been gone?"

The Indian studied the ground in front of the door. "We are still a day behind them."

Caleb headed for the door to leave. "Then we better get going."

"You need rest." Runs Swiftly answered. He walked away from the cabin and sat down.

"I need to find my wife. We'll rest when we find her." Caleb watched Runs Swiftly stretch and lean back against the bark of the tree.

Runs Swiftly tilted his head and said. "Runs Swiftly needs rest." He crossed his arms over his chest and shut his eyes.

Caleb walked back to the shack. He knelt by the door and looked for tracks. As far as he could tell, there were none. He moved further away from the shack. After searching for several minutes, Caleb became disgusted with himself. If there were any tracks, he couldn't find them.

He marched back to where Runs Swiftly reclined. The Indian rested peacefully but opened his eyes mere slits to acknowledge Caleb's presence. "Rest, friend Caleb. We will look more in the morning."

How could he rest? Caleb doubted he would sleep a wink. He sank to the ground and pressed his back against a tree. No way could he sleep in the hut. Julianne was out in these woods without protection. He prayed for her safety. Sometime during the prayer, Caleb fell asleep.

"We'll rest here for the night."

Marcus shoved Julianne into the dark, damp cave. She fell to the ground on her knees. A soft cry escaped her lips.

"How many times do I have to tell you to leave her be?" Edmond yelled as he came into the shelter.

Julianne would have laughed if she didn't hurt all over. Most of her cuts, scrapes, and bruises came from her uncle. How often today had he struck her? More than she cared to remember.

The baby gave a soft whimper.

"Marcus, get a fire going in here." Edmond rubbed his arms and looked around.

His frown spoke louder than words. Julianne cuddled the baby against her shoulder. The last thing she wanted to do was anger her uncle.

"It's not much to look at is it, Julie girl?" His gaze moved to the squirming baby in her arms.

"No, sir."

Edmond nodded his head. "Oh, I see you've remembered your manners."

Marcus dropped a pile of branches on the hard floor. "Good thing I went and got the brat, huh, boss." He knelt and began piling kindling on the ground.

The older man studied the younger. "I suppose so, but from now on you better do as I say or I won't pay you a cent."

Julianne wondered how long it would be before the two men turned on each other. From the looks of hate they exchanged it would be sooner rather than later and when that happened maybe she could escape with Jonathan.

The baby's small whimpers gained momentum.

Both men glared at her. Unless they turned their frustrations on her.

She laid him gently on the dirt floor of the cave. Julianne began to remove the blanket that concealed the baby. Several times during the day, she had thought to check on the little one but her uncle and Marcus had pushed her to keep moving.

Now that the blanket was off, Julianne gasped.

"What's wrong?" Edmond moved to her side and looked down at the baby.

It wasn't Jonathan's blue eyes that stared back at her. This baby had brown eyes, coal-black hair and tan skin.

The little fellow kicked his legs and whimpered again.

"What's the matter, girl? The baby looks fine to me." Edmond searched Julianne's face.

Julianne's heart pounded in her chest. She was amazed that her uncle and Marcus couldn't hear it. "He's hungry and I just realized we don't have any milk to feed him."

"Is that all? Well, it won't hurt him to go through one night without something to eat." Edmond straightened to his full height. He rubbed his back and then knelt down beside the fire.

Julianne sighed with relief. She felt sure her uncle would kill the baby if he knew the truth.

Her gaze met Marcus's. The dark eyebrows slanted in a frown. Had he guessed he'd taken the wrong baby? She wondered how he'd known to look for Jonathan in an Indian village. Or had he found them at the cabin? As he stared at her and his eyes hardened, Julianne silently prayed. *Lord, please don't let him figure it out.* She kept her expression under stern restraint.

The baby whimpered again. Why hadn't she noticed he hadn't cried out all day? Jonathan would have been screaming for hours, but this baby hadn't. Why?

She removed the wet animal skin that had been used as a diaper. Julianne wondered if her uncle would notice the skin and realize this was an Indian child. For safe measure, she tucked the soiled skin inside a fold in the blanket.

The baby needed a fresh diaper. Julianne stood and turned her back to the men. She pulled her dress up and tore off her chemise at the bottom, then tied it around the baby to make a diaper.

Julianne picked up the little boy and held him close. "I won't let them harm you," she whispered to the baby.

She needed to get rid of the dirty diaper. Her gaze moved to her uncle and Marcus. The men sat with their backs to her. Since they blocked the only exit out, she backed further into the darkness of the cave, keeping a watchful eye on the men.

The further she went the darker it became. Julianne continued to ease deeper into the cavern with the baby and its blanket. When she felt the wall at her back, she searched the darkness for a place to hide the soiled skin. A crack in the wall caught her attention. Once more she looked toward her uncle and Marcus.

They still weren't paying attention to her. Julianne pulled the used diaper out of the blanket and shoved it as far into the crack as she could.

"What are you doing?" Edmond barked from the entry.

Julianne came forward, "I was just looking for a place to…" She didn't know what more to say.

"Come on, I'll take you." Her uncle got to his feet. "Well, hurry up. I don't want to spend any more time out there than we need to." He headed out of the cave.

Fortunately he had misunderstood her stammer to mean she needed to relieve herself. Julianne quickly followed him.

They didn't go very far till Edmond stopped. He pointed at a clump of bushes. "Go behind there and hurry it up."

Julianne saw this as her moment to escape. It would be dark soon, and they would never find her. She took one step away, and her uncle stopped her by putting a firm hand on her shoulder.

"I'll take the baby, Julie girl."

She turned to face him. "Oh, I don't mind taking him, Uncle. I'm used to having Jonathan with me." Julianne offered what she hoped was her most innocent smile.

"That may be true, but the little one stays with me." He took the baby from her arms. "Now you hurry."

What could she do?

Frustrated at the loss of a chance at escape, Julianne did as she was told and hurried back.

Edmond handed the child to her, his eyes searching hers. "You know, I didn't think you would leave after I took the money and your ticket. You are resourceful, just like your mother." His eyes softened for a brief moment. "How did you get the money to come out here?"

For a moment, Julianne thought about her uncle's life. At one time he had been a good man with a good heart. She didn't know what had turned him into the cold, cruel man he had become. What could happen that would cause a man to turn bitter toward God and his own family?

"I came with Asa Mercer." She looked down at the baby in her arms. The little one sucked noisily on his fist.

Edmond rubbed his arms and gazed up at the stars. "They say a man can get lost in this place."

Julianne looked up at him. "We don't have to go back, Uncle Edmond. You could stay here and make a new start."

His laugh was bitter and his eyes were full of sorrow as he answered. "Not me, Julie girl. I have a family to take care of. Responsibilities." Edmond stared down at her for several long minutes. "I'm sorry, I can't return without you."

"But why, Uncle? Why must I go back with you? You

hated me living in your home. And Kassie is fifteen years old now. She can help Aunt Martha with the chores and the twins." Personally Julianne thought it might do her spoiled cousin a world of good to get her hands a little dirty with a bit of old-fashioned hard work.

"You don't understand." There was a cold edge of irony in his voice that was not lost on Julianne. "My daughters were not brought up to do manual labor. I can't afford to hire a housekeeper—that's what we kept you for. Since you ran away, there has been no one to help Martha and the community is getting suspicious about our financial standing. They must never learn that I am broke and my family almost destitute. That would ruin my daughters' chances of making desirable matches." He expelled a long audible breath. "There are no other options available. You must return with me."

Momentarily speechless in her surprise, Julianne spoke without thinking.

"Broke? Destitute?" The two words caused her mind to spin with bewilderment. Her uncle owned businesses in six different cities. His name was a household word. "What are you talking about, Uncle Edmond? You're one of the wealthiest men in New York."

"Not anymore." For a moment it seemed his eyes glimmered with visions of the past, then he regarded her with curious intensity. "And not without you." A shiver of dread slithered down her spine. What did he mean?

"Do you remember several years ago when I made that trip to the Nevada territory?"

"Yes. You went on a survey trip to investigate the possibility of building stores in the rapidly growing mining towns."

"That's right. But while there I learned some disturbing news. I tried to find a way around the law that kept me from funds I should have had access to. But your father had sewn things up tight."

Julianne felt on the edge of a precipice. She was uncertain she wanted to know what he apparently felt compelled to share. "What news, Uncle Edmond?"

"Never mind that right now, Julianne. You'll know soon enough." He glared at her for interrupting. "Anyway, while I was there and because I was so upset, I began to play in a gaming house."

Comprehension dawned and a soft gasp escaped her. "Oh, Uncle. You gambled?"

He spread his hands regretfully and shrugged.

"Quite often. And, finally, one time too many. I lost it all. The businesses, my horses, my bank account. The only thing I have left is my cattle. I'm fifty years old and starting from scratch again."

"How did Aunt Martha take the news?" Julianne thought about her proud aunt and her heart filled with compassion.

"She doesn't know, and she must never learn of this. That's why you have to go back. If you help with the household so it looks like everything is running as usual, I can earn enough money from the sale of my cattle to keep us going till I get on my feet again. It shouldn't take more than a year. You keep the secret, the baby stays safe, and then you're free to leave again. By that time your older cousins will have made good matches and everything will be back to normal. Your aunt never needs to know how close we came to ruin."

Julianne blinked in bafflement.

"When we get home, I'll need your signature on some documents."

Searching for a plausible explanation she asked, "Why would you need *my* signature?"

He stammered as he answered and a wave of apprehension swept through her. Her uncle was an acclaimed public speaker. Why, then, was he stuttering? This could not be good.

"Why, um, oh…just promise that you won't leave until the year is up." He seemed pleased with his answer but a nagging in the back of her mind refused to be still.

"How could Aunt Martha not know of your financial difficulties?" Julianne's disbelief showed in the tone of her voice. Maybe he could keep the household running as usual, but Aunt Martha loved going to the store her uncle owned in New York. If the store had a new owner, her aunt would know it.

"I told her I sold the business to fund new stores in Nevada territory. That's where she thinks I'm at right now." He leaned toward her, his voice mocking. "Imagine her surprise when I show up with you."

"Why didn't you just tell her you made a bad mistake? Aunt Martha loves you. She would have forgiven you and helped you fix this disaster. Surely the family could learn to live on less for a while. Till you recover your fortune."

His expression changed and became almost somber. He was usually a massive, self-confident presence, but at the moment his shoulders sagged as if they bore the weight of the world. Drops of moisture clung to his forehead and the age lines about his eyes and mouth carved deep into his skin.

"I couldn't bear to see the pain in her eyes that my confession would have caused. I couldn't have her think less of me as a man. First I told one lie, and then I had to lie again to cover that one. Then before I knew it I had created a web of deceit that could not be straightened out without major damage to my family. My girls would have been ashamed of their papa. We could not hold our heads up in town if everyone found out the truth."

Julianne fought hard against tears and clenched her jaw to kill the sob in her throat. How could she judge her uncle? She was guilty of the same sin. She had lied to Caleb so many times to keep her secrets. Now, she might never get the chance to say she was sorry. How could one little lie cause so much turmoil?

The baby's stomach growled loudly, and he twisted in Julianne's arms. She shifted him, placing his head against her shoulder. She looked up at her uncle, expecting the hardness to have returned to his face, but the dark eyes surveyed her kindly. It was as if confessing his faults had lightened his load. Too bad he had confessed to the wrong person. Julianne could not help him, but she knew someone who could. She opened her mouth to tell her uncle how she had accepted the Lord.

"We will talk no more, Julianne." He took her by the elbow and propelled her toward the mouth of the cave. Though she tried hard to feel no sympathy, her heart ached for her uncle. He wanted the same thing she did.

Freedom.

Freedom from the lies that had them bound. Did he not understand that accepting the Lord could set a person free? How could he not know this when he had quoted scripture to her all her life? How angry would he become if she shared with him the miracle that had happened to her.

Edmond entered the cavern, pulling Julianne along behind him. Marcus stood in the shadows at the back of the lair. Julianne bent her head to speak to the baby, but something about Marcus's stance caused her head to jerk upward again, icy fear twisting around her heart.

With a flick of his wrist, Marcus's knife flew through the air. It hit Edmond in the chest. The dull thud echoed in the cave.

Julianne screamed as her uncle fell to the ground. She dropped by his side. His hands clutched at the knife buried in his chest.

"Oh Lord, what have you done, Marcus?" She laid the baby on the ground beside her.

Marcus moved from the shadows to stand by her side. "I did what I should have done days ago." Marcus bent down and jerked the knife from Edmond's heart. He wiped the blood on his pants leg and walked toward the entrance.

"I'll be back in a few minutes. Be ready to travel."

She moved to her uncle's head and placed it on her lap. Julianne knew he didn't have long to live. Tears ran down her cheeks unchecked. He may have abused her, but at one time in her young life, Uncle Edmond had been her hero.

He looked up into her face. "I'm sorry."

"Please don't try to talk, Uncle Edmond. I'm going to get you out of here." Julianne couldn't stop the flow of tears.

He reached up and touched her swollen lips and then her eye. "No time. I never wanted to hurt you, Julie girl. Can you forgive me?" He coughed and blood trickled from the corner of his lip. "You have to go back to Martha. You'll take over the businesses and take care of the family. Promise me."

Julianne placed her hand over his. "Uncle Edmond,

don't give up. We'll get you out of here and you'll be good as new."

He coughed once more. Frantically he grasped her hand. "Promise me, Julianne."

Confused, she hesitated then blurted out, "But what businesses, Uncle Edmond? You said you lost them all."

His eyes drifted shut. "You turned eighteen, Julianne. That's how I lost them. You are now the sole owner of your father's businesses. They were never mine. I planned to steal them from you. I thought I had another year, but the day you turned eighteen the estate lawyer refused to allow any more business dealings without your signature. I pulled money from different places and came to get you."

She listened, blinking in bewilderment. Her uncle had lived off her father's wealth. She'd been treated like a slave in his home while his family lived like New York high society. But even though she felt the sting of his duplicity she still wanted him to live.

"We can work it out, Uncle Edmond. I'll sign the papers. You'll be okay." With his last breath he said. "That's not going to happen, Julie girl." His hand slid from her face and fell to the ground.

The sound of boots at the entrance of the cave announced Marcus's return. Julianne gently slid out from under her uncle. She rested his head on the ground and lifted the baby into her shaking arms. Tears blinded her and rolled down her cheeks. A flash of wild grief ripped through her. Her uncle had not treated her kindly, and most of her life she'd feared him, but he was family. And now she was alone with Marcus.

"We're leaving." Marcus grabbed his bag and the one Edmond had been carrying.

Julianne stood her ground. "I'm not going anywhere with you." She clung tightly to the baby.

Marcus growled in the back of his throat. "Yes, you are."

She shook her head at him and stepped backward.

He was on her in a heartbeat. "I said we are going." Marcus ground out the words through clinched teeth. His fingers bit into her arm as he dragged her from the cave.

"Where are you taking me?" Julianne tried to dig her feet into the cave floor.

Marcus jerked on her arm harder. "We're being followed. I'm trying to get you to safety."

Her heart leaped into her throat. She had felt that strange sense of being followed but instead of fear it had made her feel assured. Relief weakened her knees. She was tired and sore, and her heart ached. She didn't understand why she did it, but she laughed. "Get me to safety?" She fell to the ground.

He was at her side in a flash. When Julianne didn't attempt to get up, Marcus thrust the knife under her chin. "See this?"

Laughter continued to spill from her body as she rocked back and forth. "Yeah, I see it. But, I don't think you will kill me, Marcus. If you had wanted to kill me, I'd already be dead. So put that away." The words poured from her lips. Julianne wondered if exhaustion could be the reason she didn't care what he did to her now.

Marcus jerked the baby from her arms. "You're right. I plan to sell you to one of the ship captains." He turned the knife on the baby.

"No!" The word shuddered through the breath that caught in her throat. "I'll go." She added a little more calmly.

"I thought so." Marcus yanked her to her feet.

They walked for what seemed like hours, but in actuality couldn't have been more than fifteen or twenty minutes. They entered a clearing where the trees had little underbrush, and Marcus began to run at a fast clip, his tight grip on Julianne's upper arm propelling her along beside him. They ran until the underbrush thickened again and began to scratch through her long dress, tearing her petticoat. Her sides ached, and her stomach heaved. "Marcus, please, I can't run anymore."

He stopped. His gaze searched the trees. "We'll rest here—but only for a few moments." His hard eyes warned her not to try to escape.

Julianne sat down on a boulder by a large tree. In the evening dusk, she couldn't make out what type of tree it was, and she really didn't care. "Marcus, please let me have my baby back. I'll go with you."

Marcus thrust the baby into her arms and sank down at her feet. His eyes searched the woods around them.

She checked the baby to make sure he wasn't injured. He grabbed her finger and sucked on it. "Oh, you poor thing," Julianne cooed.

"Be quiet." Marcus hissed.

"Who do you think is following us?" Julianne whispered as she clutched the baby closer to her. The thought that maybe Caleb was out there made her heart quicken.

"We're not far from an Indian village. If you're a smart girl, you'll keep quiet. Haven't you heard what they do to pretty little white girls?"

Julianne had heard the stories of tribes taking captives and turning them into slaves. She'd heard many tales about horrible things the Indian men did to white women. But she also knew Morning Star, and Julianne couldn't imagine her people being that cruel. And Marcus had already proven to be an animal without any morals. How much safer did he think he made her feel?

They sat in silence for several minutes. The sounds of small animals rustling through the leaves and grass filled the evening air.

Julianne tucked the baby's blanket around her shoulders and cuddled him close to keep him warm.

"Marcus, why did you kill my uncle?"

Her question seemed to amuse him. "Why do you think?"

"I don't know. I thought you would let him live, at least until he paid you." She patted the baby's back.

"I guess it won't hurt none to tell you. While you were out, I checked his bag and found it full of money." He sneered then chuckled. "Your money, as it is. I didn't need him anymore." Marcus tipped his head and looked up into the foliage that was blocking what little light was left of the evening.

Julianne's tired mind spun with questions. So Marcus knew she had money. Businesses. He wasn't going to sell her; he was going to demand a ransom. How could Marcus kill in cold blood? How many times had he killed? She knew he would have killed her already, if he didn't think her family would pay handsomely for her.

"Why do you say it's my money?"

"Your uncle tried to convince your aunt to sign the papers releasing the inheritance from your parents. He told her he'd had word from you and that you wanted to come home." He gave an evil grunt. "But you'd come of age and she couldn't sign any longer. Now neither of you will return home."

"But you didn't have to kill him."

"What do you care anyway?" He sneered. "He killed your pa and ma, and soon as he had your signature on those papers he planned to kill you, too. 'Sides it wasn't like he was yer fav'rit uncle or nothing. He slapped you around."

Julianne rocked the baby from side to side. "He was my uncle." But even as she said it she wondered if Marcus was telling the truth about her uncle killing her parents. Could he have been so evil?

Marcus laughed, "Yeah, he told me he didn't think you had it in ya to run off the way you did. Especially since he stole all yer money."

"I forgive him for that. I would have loved to have seen him make it back home to my aunt and cousins."

"Now don't ya go spouting that religious stuff ta me 'bout forgiveness. I tried me that when I married my first wife. So purdy she was and loved to go to Sunday meeting. I thought about it and figgered it was a better way of life than my pa had, so I started going with her to the services." He leaned his head back against the tree.

"But the whole time I was a-trying to live better, she was seeing another man. Ever' day she told me she had to drive just outside town to tend her sick mama, but it was all lies. She left on the stage one day with the preacher man. That's when I found out. Decided right then and there that there'd be no more religion fer me. No sirree."

Julianne saw a frown settle deep into his features and sought for a plausible answer to soothe the anger, betrayal and hurt she knew lay buried in this man's soul. It did not escape her tired mind that, once again, lies had taken away a person's happiness, leaving in their place an empty, broken shell. She'd noticed that with each word he spoke, Marcus dropped more letters in words. It was as if he was reliving a time when he'd been younger.

She pulled her thoughts back to the problem at hand. What could she say to him? Her uncle was dead but there was still a chance for her and Marcus to grow whole again. "Marcus, when you tried out religion with your wife, did you give your heart to the Lord?" Julianne kept her voice low and purposefully nonchalant.

"Naw, I reckon not. I was a-workin' up to it, but when Daisy left it came to me that ever'thing she ever said about religious stuff was pro'bly a lie, just like all the other stuff that came outta her mouth. Since that day, I been a-takin' what I wanted and killing anything that got in my way."

A hand, massive and strong, clamped down on her knee.

"And I be a'thinkin that it's time I take what you got to offer, and I don't mean no religion."

Julianne stiffened, bracing herself for the fight she knew approached like a raging fire. She cast a fearful look down at Marcus. She gasped.

A snake wound around through the foliage of the tree he leaned against. He turned his head to see what had captured her attention and yelped in fear. Alarmed by the sudden movement and noise, the snake sank its fangs into his neck and would not let go.

Julianne jumped off the boulder and ran, clutching the baby against her chest.

Chapter 16

Caleb couldn't believe his eyes. The scene in front of him seemed to unfold in slow motion.

The snake coiled around Marcus's shoulders then slithered to the ground. Runs Swiftly threw his knife and pinned the snake's head to the ground with the tip of the blade.

Julianne tripped over a branch and stumbled, just managing to catch herself from falling. She cradled the baby against her. Caleb watched her eyes widen as he ran to her. Her face turned ashen and she fainted into his arms. He lowered her gently to the ground.

Runs Swiftly left Marcus to his own devices and came to stand beside Caleb. "She is hurt?"

The baby let out a soft whimper and Runs Swiftly lifted the infant from the tangled folds of Julianne's dress.

Caleb knelt beside Julianne. Her bottom lip was

bruised and cracked. A small trickle of blood had dried in the corner. One eye was swollen. He quickly ran his hands over her arms and legs. "I don't think she has any serious injuries." He smiled up at Runs Swiftly, thankfulness winging its way through his veins.

The Indian man stood, holding the baby Julianne had carried. His face paled and his dark eyes blinked with disbelief.

"What's wrong?"

Runs Swiftly raised his head and stared down at Julianne. "Your woman had Little Eagle."

Marcus moaned, drawing the men's attention.

Runs Swiftly gently placed the infant in Caleb's arms. He walked to the snake and pulled his knife out of the reptile's head. In one swift motion he ended Marcus's suffering then turned back toward Julianne.

Caleb saw the anger and mistrust in his friend's eyes. He quickly stood to his feet and braced to protect Julianne.

Runs Swiftly stopped and extended his arms for the child. The baby whimpered as Caleb handed the child back.

"I don't understand, Runs Swiftly."

Caleb watched the softening in the expression on the warrior's face as he gazed down at the infant, then his features became more animated.

"I must get Little Eagle back to my sister. You will care for your wife alone?"

"You're leaving me?" Puzzled by the abrupt change in Runs Swiftly's mood, Caleb's brain failed to comprehend what he had said.

Sure that Julianne was no longer in danger, Caleb

returned to her side. He smoothed the hair from her forehead.

"While you slept in the night, Mountain Boy, from our village came with the news that our village was attacked yesterday. Our warriors were out on a hunt and only the older men were in camp. Several of them were wounded and my sister's baby, Little Eagle, was taken. My tribe will be happy to see that this child lives."

Caleb had been aware of Runs Swiftly's silence most of the day. Now he knew why. "I'm sorry. But, surely you know that Julianne would never have taken part in something like that."

"No, I believe the man did it." Runs Swiftly carried the baby to his horse. "Little Eagle needs his mother's milk." He mounted the horse in one swift motion and turned to go. "Morning Star will bring your son to you."

"Thank you."

The Indian nodded and left.

Julianne groaned. One eye opened slowly. The swollen eye remained shut. She focused on his face and began to cry.

"It's okay, sweetheart. You're safe now."

She struggled to sit up. Her hands touched his cheeks. "You're alive?"

Caleb laughed with relief. "Of course, I'm alive."

"Marcus said…" Her gaze jerked to the tree where Marcus's still body lay. "Is he…?"

He turned her face toward him. "He's dead."

As if she suddenly remembered, Julianne frantically searched the ground around her. "The baby, where's the baby?" Tears formed as she searched the area for the child.

"Julianne." Caleb drew her attention back to himself.

When he was sure he had her full attention once more he continued. "The baby is fine. Runs Swiftly just left with him. He needs nourishment."

Julianne cradled his face in trembling hands. "I thought you were dead. My uncle said he would kill the baby if I didn't go with him. Marcus killed my uncle."

Caleb pulled her to him. "I know." His gaze moved to Marcus. What kind of man threatened and hurt a woman? It was a question that would never be answered for him. He pulled his wife into his embrace and held her tight.

His gentle hands rubbed her back. His warm voice soothed, offering words of comfort, while his heart beat strongly under her cheek. Julianne clung to his shirt. Deep sobs racked her insides, fear and anxiety slowly releasing their tenacious holds on her body. Her tears drenched the front of his shirt. She didn't ever want to leave his protective arms. Now that they were together again, Julianne decided she never wanted to be where Caleb was not.

When he scooped her up and stood, Julianne wrapped her arms around his neck, her face resting against his jaw. At the base of his throat a pulse beat and swelled as though his heart had risen from its usual place. She placed her lips against it, and it made her feel good. She was so glad to be with him.

"Let's go home." Caleb carried her to the horse that waited under a nearby tree.

"Home," she sighed. Her body ached and her eyelids felt heavy.

Caleb stood beside the animal. "Sweetheart, we have to get on the horse."

What if this was a dream? It had to be a dream. Caleb

had never called her sweetheart. What if he wasn't real? Fear caused her to tighten her grip around his neck. "Don't leave me, Caleb."

"I'm not going to leave you." He hugged her close, his breath fanning her cheek. He brushed a gentle kiss across her forehead.

The warmth in his voice assured her. She released her hold on him. He set her down on the ground and made a stirrup with his hands. She put one foot in his hand and allowed him to give her a lift up onto the horse.

"Caleb, would you get my uncle's personal belongings? They are over there." She pointed to where Marcus lay. "I want to send them home to my aunt."

He nodded. He retrieved the bags and handed them to her. Caleb swung up behind her and took the rope in his hands, resting his arms on each side of her. She placed the bags across her lap.

Julianne leaned back against him and enjoyed his warmth and strength. If this was a dream, she prayed she'd never wake up.

"We'll be home soon," he assured her.

She felt as though she was forgetting something, but her tired mind refused to focus. The warmth of Caleb surrounded and comforted her. Sleep pulled at her. Her eyelids grew heavy.

Then she remembered.

Julianne sat up and pulled away from Caleb's embrace. "Oh, Caleb. Where is Jonathan?" she cried.

He gently pulled her back against him. "Jonathan is fine. Morning Star has him. Don't worry, he's safe, Julianne."

"You met Morning Star?" Dread filled her tired mind. She had wanted to be the one to tell him everything.

More tears ran silently down her face. "I'm sorry," she whispered.

He placed his head on top of hers. "So am I, Julianne."

Julianne couldn't fight the fatigue any longer. She was frozen in limbo where all decisions and actions were impossible to make. She was aware that Caleb spoke softly to her, but his words didn't register in her dizzied senses. Gradually his voice drifted into a hushed whisper and she fell asleep in his arms.

Caleb cradled his wife against him. Even dirty, she smelled of lavender. He rested his head on hers and inhaled deeply. He silently thanked the Lord for her safety.

By the time they reached the cabin, the first streaks of dawn spanned out over the heavens, pinkish in hue.

He was tired and sore, but he had to admit he was a happy man. His wife was safe and resting in his arms.

As he rode into the yard, Maggie ran out to meet him. "I'm so glad you're back! I have been worried sick."

He nuzzled Julianne's hair one last time. "Sweetheart, wake up. We're home."

She stirred in his arms, and then snuggled deeper into his chest.

"How is she?" Maggie stood beside the horse looking up at them.

Caleb shifted Julianne's weight. "She's tired. I don't think she's slept at all in the last five days."

"We'll have her in her nice warm bed in no time." Maggie's loud voice carried on the morning mists.

Julianne pulled herself from the deep sleep. She straightened up and looked down at Maggie. Then she burst into tears.

"Now, now, let's get you down from there." Maggie

soothed, as Caleb pulled the bags off Julianne's lap and
handed them to Maggie, who set them on the ground.
Then, he lowered Julianne until she was within Maggie's warm embrace.

As soon as her feet touched soil, Julianne fell into
Maggie's arms and sobbed. "It was awful, Maggie."

The older woman drew her into the house. "I'm sure
it was, child." She made a couple of clicking noises with
her tongue.

"What you need is a nice, hot bath." She eased Julianne into the rocker and headed outside for the washtub.

Julianne kept a tight rein on her thoughts refusing
to think about the last few days. She looked around the
cabin and silently thanked God she was safe from harm.
Everything took on a deeper meaning. The love of her
peaceful home, the care Caleb had given her since the
first day he married her and the cradle next to her bed.
Caleb and Jonathan were her life and what a blessed
life it was.

Maggie dragged the metal bathtub into the kitchen.
"Caleb's taking care of the livestock and said he'd be in
later." She went back outside, returned with Julianne's
belongings and set them to the side of the door.

"I'll help bring in the water." Julianne stood slowly.
Every muscle in her body ached. A soak in hot water
would do her a world of good.

"You'll do no such thing. There's fresh coffee on the
stove. Why don't you pour us a cup? I'll get the water
going, and then you can tell me all about your adven-
tures."

Julianne limped to the stove and filled two cups with
hot coffee as Maggie carried the water inside. While the
water heated Julianne told Maggie about her uncle and

her life before she came to Washington. Then she told Maggie about the abduction and the time that she'd spent with Marcus and her uncle.

Maggie poured the heated water into the tub and crossed the room to the door. "Well, it's all over now, and you're home safe. I'm going to go check on that man of yours. It's time I tell him I was wrong and you aren't expecting a wee one any time soon." She closed the door behind her.

The warm water relieved Julianne's aches, but tiredness enveloped her as she tried to think. She'd lost weight. She felt drained, hollow and lifeless. She scrubbed the horror of the days away. Pain seeped from her body, and her eyes grew drowsy once more.

After a long soak, she finally felt human enough to get out of the tub. Dressed in her nightgown, she walked slowly to the bed and decided to lie down for a few minutes. She crawled into the big bed and pulled the quilt over her shoulders. Soon she was fast asleep, but her dreams tormented her. She was being chased. Someone threatened to kill Jonathan. A face lingered around the edges of her mind, torturing her. She remembered keen, probing eyes. There was blood everywhere, and though she tried hard, she couldn't get it off her hands. She was trapped. Suddenly, the image focused in her memory. Marcus. She screamed and sat straight up in the bed.

"Shhh. I'm here now. You're safe, sweetheart." Caleb's soothing voice penetrated the horror. Large hands took her face and held it gently. "It was a nightmare." His hands slipped to her shoulders, and he pulled her against him. Gathering her into his arms he held her snugly.

Julianne buried her face against the corded muscles

of his chest, and the trembling in her body slowly subsided. She began to relax as he rocked her back and forth.

Sometime later she woke sore and disoriented. The soft sounds of Caleb's snores comforted her. Until she realized they were beside her instead of overhead.

Turning on her side to face him, she studied his profile. His features were softened in sleep. Mentally, she reviewed his qualities. He had searched for her, all the while thinking she'd betrayed him with another man. She'd slept in his arms on the ride home, and he'd kissed her hair and whispered endearments. He had unlocked her heart and soul and every day her love for him had deepened and intensified.

In her dreams he had come and saved her from Marcus. Had he really been talking to her last night? Told her she was safe? In her heart, she knew he had.

Julianne's gaze moved to the cradle. Caleb had said the baby was with Morning Star. Did he know how she'd met the Indian woman? Was he aware that she'd done the loggers' laundry for the last couple of months?

She slipped from the bed. Her legs were stiff and sore. Ignoring the pain, she moved to the little wooden box. Julianne eased the lid open and looked at the money. If she hadn't done the last batch of laundry, would her uncle have found her?

Now that he was dead, Julianne realized she no longer had to fear or lie. She could be a real wife to Caleb and a real mother to Jonathan. She closed the lid on the box. Would Caleb want a real wife? Or was he happy with things the way they were?

"How do you feel?"

Julianne jumped. When had he awakened? She turned to Caleb and looked through one eye. "I'm sore."

He sat up and rubbed his eyes.

Julianne carried the little wooden box to the bed and sat down on the edge. "I'm sorry, Caleb."

Caleb raised his head. His gaze fell to the box. Was she going to tell him about the money now? Or was she going to tell him she was leaving? He swallowed the lump that suddenly developed in his throat.

He'd heard Marcus confess that her uncle had taken the money for her passage to Washington. And now, with her uncle dead, Julianne had no reason to stay with him. She no longer needed his protection.

"So am I."

"There are so many things I need to tell you."

He watched her rub the lid of the box. Caleb scooted off the bed. "You don't have to tell me anything. With your uncle gone, you don't need my protection anymore. I won't hold you to the marriage, Julianne." He pulled his boots on over clean socks.

"You don't want to be married to me?" Her voice was barely above a whisper.

He shut his eyes and kept his head down, knowing that hurt and longing would be naked in his eyes. "Without your uncle threatening you, I'd think you would be ready to move on."

He hurt.

His chest hurt, his throat hurt, but most of all the pain in his heart left him empty. He couldn't meet her gaze.

"I see." Julianne dumped the money on the bed. "So I scrubbed other men's dirty clothes for nothing." He heard the bitterness in her voice.

What was she talking about? Caleb raised his head and saw the money on the bed.

Julianne jerked her bag out from under the bed. "I'll leave here with nothing more than what I brought with me. I thought you might learn to love me, Caleb Hansen. I thought you wanted to start an apple orchard and a family with me. I'm such a fool." Her words were loaded with self-ridicule and held a tinge of sourness.

"I'm giving you your freedom." His eyes stung. Why was she acting as though he'd done something wrong?

She stopped shoving clothes in the bag and turned to face him. "Why?"

The whispered question hung between them.

He took a step closer to her. "I thought that was what you wanted."

"Why would I want to leave the only man I ever loved? I have washed clothes three times a week since I married you to raise money. First, I thought it was to pay you back the money you paid Sloan. Then, it became a way to make your dream come true. To start the apple orchard."

He took another step forward. "You did that for me? You love me?"

At her half nod Caleb swept her into his arms.

He buried his face in her hair. He tightened his hold as she clung to him.

After long moments, he drew away so he could look into her eyes.

"Julianne, I didn't realize how much I loved you until you were gone. I thought I would go out of my mind when I realized someone had taken you from me." He rained kisses across her forehead, his hands encircling her neck. "I never want to lose you again. You have become my life, my reason for being." He cupped her face in his hands and gently kissed her. When he pulled away, he whispered against her lips, "My best friend."

"Then don't send me away." She covered his hands with hers. "I never want to be apart from you again."

"This is more than I ever dared hope for." Caleb seemed to search for words to explain what he meant. "To love you this much is a powerful feeling, but to have you love me back the same way is wonderful beyond words. It's almost…"

"Spiritual?"

"Yes!" he exclaimed huskily. "I feel spiritually married to you."

She wrapped her arms around his neck and he enclosed her in a tight hug. He felt her trembling and drew back in remorse.

"Oh, Julianne, I'm sorry. You should be in bed resting and here I am tiring you out." He smoothed the covers back and lifted her into the bed.

She clung to his hand, refusing to let him go. "You've had a rough several days, too."

His heart felt as though it might explode. He lay beside her and wrapped her securely in his arms.

Chapter 17

They woke together. She stretched, and her stomach growled noisily.

"I'm hungry."

"You're hungry."

They spoke simultaneously and Julianne giggled like a child. She felt ravenous. She went to the kitchen, placed a cast-iron pan on the stove and then realized all the food in the house would have spoiled by now.

"Caleb, will you get us a slab of meat from the smokehouse?" She turned and squealed as Caleb swept her off her feet depositing her back in the bed.

"You stay put." He chucked her under the chin, his head came down and he kissed her gently.

Caleb groaned. "Woman, quit tempting me." He stepped away from her, their hands still linked together as if impossible to separate. "I need sustenance. Now be good and I'll serve you supper in a jiffy."

"Supper?"

Julianne's gaze shot to the window in the living room and she realized the sun shone on the western side of the house. They had slept away the day.

"Oh, Caleb, I have to get dressed. Morning Star will be here any minute with Jonathan." She slipped from the bed and crossed to the nightstand that sat beside her bed. She poured water in the basin, dipped a cloth and began to wash her face.

Warm hands slid around her waist, and she leaned back into Caleb's hug.

"Just take it easy, sweetheart. I don't want anything happening to my girl. You've had a rough week. You need time to recuperate. Promise me."

"I promise."

Julianne turned into his embrace, savoring the feel of his strong arms. She stood on tiptoe and touched her lips to his.

She stared until the door closed behind him, then in a flurry of motion, finished her toilet, made the bed, and put on a pot of water to boil. Minutes later, she dropped sliced potatoes into the water and placed a lid on the top. She would fry whatever meat Caleb brought in, and they'd have stewed potatoes and relish.

They had just finished their meal when a low whistle sounded outside. Julianne rushed to the door but Caleb got there first, pulling the heavy door wide.

Morning Star and Runs Swiftly stood at the bottom of the porch steps, huge grins on their faces. Julianne reached out eagerly for the bundle in Morning Star's arms and almost fell down the steps in her hurry to get him. Only Caleb's quick response saved her from the fall.

Julianne's arms encircled Morning Star and Jonathan at the same time. They ended up in an awkward hug, tears of joy filling their eyes.

"Oh, Morning Star. I'm so happy to see you."

Caleb clasped hands with Runs Swiftly as Julianne pulled Morning Star up the steps into the house.

Both men followed on the women's heels as if unwilling to let them out of their sight. Grateful for how safe and wanted such attention made her feel, Julianne touched Caleb's hand, hoping to silently convey her acceptance and joy at his hovering.

Julianne kissed Jonathan's cheek then snuggled him close to her breast. She breathed in his warm, baby scent, her heart rejoicing that the Lord had protected him.

She spoke to him in soft, gentle words, and he stilled as if listening to her voice. When he grinned suddenly, she gasped and glanced quickly at Caleb to see if he noticed.

She shared a look of love with him and he stepped closer, his arm slipping around her waist. Julianne dared to look at Morning Star again and found a knowing smile on her friend's face.

"How are Little Eagle and his mother?" Caleb asked Runs Swiftly.

"My sister sent you this as a token of her thanks." He pulled an object from the pouch he carried over his shoulder and handed it to Julianne.

She unwrapped a beautiful leather papoose. "This will make it so much easier to carry Jonathan around. The sheet was so bulky."

Julianne smoothed a hand over the soft leather. "But I have no gift for you, and you have done so much for me."

"No gift important." Morning Star placed a hand

against Julianne's heart. "Friend important. We have news."

She reached up and took Runs Swiftly's hand. He placed the other hand on her shoulder, a look of pure devotion on his face. "Six full moons, we have child."

Julianne swept her friend into a fierce hug, knowing that had been the desire of Morning Star's heart since she lost her first baby in childbirth.

"God has truly blessed us, Morning Star."

"Someday soon, you must tell me about this God and how he can bless us, but now we must return to our tribe." Runs Swiftly nodded to both Julianne and Caleb. He took Morning Star's hand and pulled her outside to his awaiting horse.

As they stepped out on the porch, Julianne was overcome with thankfulness that Morning Star was alive and that she had taken such good care of Jonathan.

"Wait." Her voice came out firm and strong. "I *do* have something for you."

She handed Jonathan to Caleb and hurried into the cabin. She returned to the porch and placed her wooden box in Morning Star's hands.

"Caleb made me this box, and I love it, but it's become a symbol of something I never want in my home again. It's so lovely, and his work is perfect. That's why I can't give it to anyone else. I know you will treasure it as I do."

Morning Star opened the box and gasped at the money inside. "Friend. Why you give thing so close to your heart?"

"Because we are starting anew, and I want Caleb to build a hope chest as a reminder of the hope God has granted us this week."

"Then I give many thanks, friend." Morning Star closed the lid, handed the box up to Runs Swiftly and allowed him to pull her up onto the horse.

Julianne stood with Caleb and watched their friends leave.

"Do you mind that I gave the box away?" Julianne felt strongly that it had been the right thing to do, and even felt relieved that the thing that had symbolized so many problems no longer sat in her house.

But Caleb might feel otherwise, and that troubled her heart somewhat. With the Lord's help, she would never again let lies and deceit get a foothold in her home.

"I don't mind at all. Actually I feel the same way about the box, but woman, did you have to give the money away, too?"

Julianne heard the humor in his voice before she glanced up and caught the merriment shining in his lovely eyes.

She raised her hand to playfully slap at him. He ducked and ran into the house. She followed. He placed Jonathan in the cradle.

Caleb grabbed her and swung her off her feet round and round several times. "You gave away my apple orchard and now you have to pay the piper."

He stopped suddenly and studied her seriously.

"I am in such trouble." He spoke in an odd, yet gentle tone.

"What do you mean?"

"I just realized that my wife gave away two months' worth of pay, and I'm happy about it." He ran a finger down her cheek. "Does that mean I'm henpecked and that you can get away with anything?"

Julianne leaned toward him, needing to impress upon him the earnestness of what she felt.

"No, Caleb. It means we are both deeply in love and wish to please each other. It means we pledge to protect our love from all that might harm our home and family. We will tell each other the truth, even if it hurts."

They stared at each other and an understanding of the vulnerable position they were in passed between them, sealing their bond of love. Julianne knew he held her happiness in his hands, and from what Caleb just admitted he felt the same way.

He took her hand and raised it to his lips.

"I love you, Mrs. Hansen."

"And I love you, Mr. Hansen."

"Just so we're clear, though, I am the boss and there is still this matter of payment you owe for giving away our money."

He pulled her to him with a slow, secret smile she fully understood.

"Oh, but you're so mistaken, boss." She place a hand on his chest, her lips just inches from his. "I did *not* give away *our* apple orchard."

"But I saw the money in the box when you handed it to Morning Star." He protested as she walked to the kitchen.

"Close your eyes," she commanded as he followed her.

"What?'

"I said close your eyes."

He lifted a brow but complied with her request when he saw the threat in her stance. She dumped the contents of something on the table. "Now open your eyes."

Caleb complied.

"What on earth? Where did you get all this money?" His smile was eager and alive with affection and delight.

Julianne's heart took wings that no doubt or mistrust showed in his eyes.

"This is the money that my uncle took from my inheritance to pay Marcus."

She set the other bag on the table and opened the top showing him another hefty number of bills. "This was my uncle's bag that Marcus stole."

She hesitated for a moment, and then her confidence spiraled upward. "If it's all right with you, I'd like us to keep the money, but I'd like to send some back to my aunt."

"But how did you get these?"

"Silly, you brought them home. Maggie carried them in, remember?"

Caleb nodded. He fingered a bundle of bills, scaling his thumb over the lot.

"How much do you think there is?"

"Enough to add a few rooms to the house and start an apple orchard."

"How do you plan to get the money back to your aunt?"

"I don't."

"What does that mean?"

"I plan to send a telegram explaining what happened and if she wants the money, she can come and get it. If I know my aunt, she is so embarrassed at their circumstances she will jump at the chance to leave New York. The sale of her house and livestock will more than pay the fare out here for her and the girls, and then this money will help set her up in her own business here."

Julianne loved the way his gaze caressed her face. She didn't much care for the frown he wore, though.

"But will you enjoy having them close by? If they treated you like your uncle did, why would you subject yourself to that again?"

"I have so much, Caleb. A husband I love with all my heart and who loves me in return. My aunt never had that. My uncle loved his businesses," she paused, "actually my father's businesses, far more than he loved his wife."

Julianne fingered the money then moved close to her husband. "You know, at some point we will have to go back and tie up the loose ends of my father's businesses—my inheritance."

"Yes, I figured as much."

"I will ask my aunt to bring what information she can from the lawyers and then we will know where we stand."
"You're that certain your aunt will come here?"

"If she wants this money she will have to. Otherwise, I will have to take it to her myself. Is that what you want?"

"Absolutely not! Woman, don't say things like that. I'm not letting you out of my sight, and now that we have this money, I think I'll order one of those new-fangled wringer washers so my wife never has to leave our yard."

"Now there's an idea, Mr. Hansen. While you're at it, how about ordering one of those treadle sewing machines?"

"Anything you say, sweetheart, as long as you're here to love me when I come home each day." The smoldering flame she saw in his eyes sent her heart spiraling out of control.

"Our hearts are in perfect harmony then, because I never want you far from me, either." Julianne could not stop herself from reaching out to touch him. He took her hand and placed it on his heart.

"You will always have a shelter in my heart, Julianne. I will always love you."

She felt his heart beating in perfect harmony with hers. She was home and all was right with the world.

* * * * *

REQUEST YOUR FREE BOOKS!

2 FREE INSPIRATIONAL NOVELS
PLUS 2
FREE
MYSTERY GIFTS

Love Inspired®

YES! Please send me 2 FREE Love Inspired® novels and my 2 FREE mystery gifts (gifts are worth about $10). After receiving them, if I don't wish to receive any more books, I can return the shipping statement marked "cancel." If I don't cancel, I will receive 6 brand-new novels every month and be billed just $4.74 per book in the U.S. or $5.24 per book in Canada. That's a savings of at least 21% off the cover price. It's quite a bargain! Shipping and handling is just 50¢ per book in the U.S. and 75¢ per book in Canada.* I understand that accepting the 2 free books and gifts places me under no obligation to buy anything. I can always return a shipment and cancel at any time. Even if I never buy another book, the two free books and gifts are mine to keep forever.

105/305 IDN F49N

Name _____ (PLEASE PRINT) _____

Address _____ Apt. #

City _____ State/Prov. _____ Zip/Postal Code

Signature (if under 18, a parent or guardian must sign)

Mail to the Harlequin® Reader Service:
IN U.S.A.: P.O. Box 1867, Buffalo, NY 14240-1867
IN CANADA: P.O. Box 609, Fort Erie, Ontario L2A 5X3

**Are you a subscriber to Love Inspired books
and want to receive the larger-print edition?
Call 1-800-873-8635 or visit www.ReaderService.com.**

* Terms and prices subject to change without notice. Prices do not include applicable taxes. Sales tax applicable in N.Y. Canadian residents will be charged applicable taxes. Offer not valid in Quebec. This offer is limited to one order per household. Not valid for current subscribers to Love Inspired books. All orders subject to credit approval. Credit or debit balances in a customer's account(s) may be offset by any other outstanding balance owed by or to the customer. Please allow 4 to 6 weeks for delivery. Offer available while quantities last.

Your Privacy—The Harlequin® Reader Service is committed to protecting your privacy. Our Privacy Policy is available online at www.ReaderService.com or upon request from the Harlequin Reader Service.
We make a portion of our mailing list available to reputable third parties that offer products we believe may interest you. If you prefer that we not exchange your name with third parties, or if you wish to clarify or modify your communication preferences, please visit us at www.ReaderService.com/consumerschoice or write to us at Harlequin Reader Service Preference Service, P.O. Box 9062, Buffalo, NY 14269. Include your complete name and address.

LIDIR13R

REQUEST YOUR FREE BOOKS!

2 FREE INSPIRATIONAL NOVELS
PLUS 2
FREE
MYSTERY GIFTS

Love Inspired.
HISTORICAL
INSPIRATIONAL HISTORICAL ROMANCE

YES! Please send me 2 FREE Love Inspired® Historical novels and my 2 FREE mystery gifts (gifts are worth about $10). After receiving them, if I don't wish to receive any more books, I can return the shipping statement marked "cancel." If I don't cancel, I will receive 4 brand-new novels every month and be billed just $4.74 per book in the U.S. or $5.24 per book in Canada. That's a savings of at least 21% off the cover price. It's quite a bargain! Shipping and handling is just 50¢ per book in the U.S. and 75¢ per book in Canada.* I understand that accepting the 2 free books and gifts places me under no obligation to buy anything. I can always return a shipment and cancel at any time. Even if I never buy another book, the two free books and gifts are mine to keep forever.

102/302 IDN F5CY

Name _____ ·(PLEASE PRINT)

Address _____ Apt. #

City _____ State/Prov. _____ Zip/Postal Code

Signature (if under 18, a parent or guardian must sign)

Mail to the Harlequin® Reader Service:
IN U.S.A.: P.O. Box 1867, Buffalo, NY 14240-1867
IN CANADA: P.O. Box 609, Fort Erie, Ontario L2A 5X3

Want to try two free books from another series?
Call 1-800-873-8635 or visit www.ReaderService.com.

* Terms and prices subject to change without notice. Prices do not include applicable taxes. Sales tax applicable in N.Y. Canadian residents will be charged applicable taxes. Offer not valid in Quebec. This offer is limited to one order per household. Not valid for current subscribers to Love Inspired Historical books. All orders subject to credit approval. Credit or debit balances in a customer's account(s) may be offset by any other outstanding balance owed by or to the customer. Please allow 4 to 6 weeks for delivery. Offer available while quantities last.

Your Privacy—The Harlequin® Reader Service is committed to protecting your privacy. Our Privacy Policy is available online at www.ReaderService.com or upon request from the Harlequin Reader Service.

We make a portion of our mailing list available to reputable third parties that offer products we believe may interest you. If you prefer that we not exchange your name with third parties, or if you wish to clarify or modify your communication preferences, please visit us at www.ReaderService.com/consumerchoice or write to us at Harlequin Reader Service Preference Service, P.O. Box 9062, Buffalo, NY 14269. Include your complete name and address.

LIHDIR13R